# Hell Train: Green Line

Kal Spriggs

# Contents

1. Chapter 1     1

2. Chapter 2     10

3. Chapter 3     17

4. Chapter 4     27

5. Chapter 5     37

6. Chapter 6     47

7. Chapter 7     59

8. Chapter 8     67

9. Chapter 9     77

10. Chapter 10     88

11. Chapter 11     98

12. Chapter 12     105

13. Chapter 13     117

14. Chapter 14     131

15. Chapter 15     143

16. Chapter 16     159

About the Author     166

Also by Kal Spriggs     167

More from Cannon Publishing      169

More From the Fae Wars      198

# Chapter One

As THE TREES TRIED to eat him, Jack wished he had brought the chainsaw.

The morning hadn't started this way. It had been sunny, and quiet, and actually rather peaceful. They hadn't seen one of the undead in days, not since the outskirts of St. Louis.

Despite Katie's protests, he had decided to go with one of the recon trucks, up the tracks, ahead of the train. There wasn't a need for him to go. He was the leader of their band of survivors. This was a routine scout-ahead to see if there were any obstacles on the track, any damage to the tracks themselves, or anything else that might derail their train.

There hadn't been any signs of threats, not since his final encounter in St. Louis, when he had introduced a terrible demonic thing to the wonders of high explosives.

In fact, after almost a year surviving in the hellish, post-apocalyptic world, Jack was positively *itching* for something to happen.

That was why he had told his second-in-command, Josh Wachope, that he would join Brian Gnad's team on recon. He felt uneasy that *nothing* had happened in the past week. Seven days of trees, quiet, and the rumble of the train without any panicked screams, shouts, or attacks left him feeling downright jittery.

In the post-apocalyptic nightmare that they lived in, this wasn't how things worked. The East Coast had drowned in millions of undead possessed. People couldn't go an hour, much less a day without something or someone trying to kill them. That was why Jack led his train full of survivors towards the west. There were fewer people out there and they were more spread out. From the limited ham radio transmissions, it sounded like survivors were more plentiful in the west.

Of course, getting there had been the challenge. Most of the highways were choked with stalled vehicles. Fuel was hard to find outside the cities. On foot, survivors could be run-down by possessed, as the undead didn't tire, didn't slow.

They had needed defenses that they could bring with them. Jack and a survivor named Paul Montandon, had worked to bring a train engine and a first few freight cars back to life, with salvaged diesel and scavenged parts.

In the time since, the survivors he led had increased as well, and now they had three train engines, rail and utility trucks for reconnaissance, and more than fifty freight cars that carried his survivors.

All of which made Jack feel that, at least sometimes, he needed to get away from the weight of responsibility and lead a recon. Besides, the last two teams had come back, part of why they had stopped south of St. Louis, because they'd run into such foul weather that they hadn't been able to continue.

As he came up to Brian's truck, he scowled as he saw Sean McCune trying to slip something into the bed. "McCune... is that a chainsaw?"

"Uh... well, that is..." McCune looked a lot like a kid whose hand had been caught in the cookie jar. "We got a whole crate of them, and it's an electric powered one, so it's pretty quiet, and I *really* want to see what it could do to one of the possessed."

"Put it away, McCune," Jack sighed.

McCune frowned, "But, *Captain*... it's battery-powered, it's Milwaukee-brand, these things are sweet! They're quiet, too, and..."

"Put it away, McCune, we don't need a chainsaw, we're just doing a bit of recon," Jack growled.

"*Fine,* Captain," Sean McCune growled. "Larry gets to have all the fun, first the booze, now he gets to keep the chainsaws."

Jack wasn't *entirely* certain what he meant by that. Larry Southard was Sean's constant companion; the two of them were some of Jack's best scroungers. They regularly found all kinds of good stuff. He could only assume that Larry and Sean had found the chainsaws and that "put it back" meant Sean McCune would give the chainsaw back to the other scavenger.

Jack went and climbed into the passenger seat of Brian's truck. Brian gave him a look, "You know, I might very well have a use for that chainsaw."

"Yeah, but McCune wasn't giving it to you, he was hiding it in the back of your truck, there's a difference," Jack answered.

Brian wasn't swayed, "If we end up needing it, he's going to say I told you so."

"He can take a number and stand in line, right behind everyone who said it was a lousy idea stepping up to lead this crazy train," Jack grumbled. "Once our favorite scrounger gets back, let's roll."

"Second-favorite," Brian told him in a prim tone. "I like Larry better; he always sets aside something for me when I'm out."

Jack rolled his eyes at that. He liked both of the scroungers, to be fair. He didn't entirely *trust* them, they *were* scroungers after all, they had a tendency to grab anything that wasn't nailed to the ground. Trust them in a fight, sure. Trust them with his life, absolutely. Though to trust them around any precious commodities or booze... well, that was something else entirely.

"Alright, I'm back," McCune grumbled as he climbed into the back seat. "Why do I have to ride back here, anyway?"

"Captain's in charge," Lieutenant Stephanie Baxter answered crisply. "That means, he rides up front." Baxter was a signal officer and she ran their radios, she carried multiple different sets with her, even now and Jack knew she'd be searching different frequencies from the point that they left the train until they got back. She could also wield the machete she wore on her hip with zero hesitation and Jack had seen her disable possessed with sharp, efficient strokes.

"Yeah, yeah," McCune grumbled. He didn't argue further, for obvious reasons.

3

Warrant Officer Tom Knighton, the fourth member of their team had put his head back and fallen asleep in the middle. Jack didn't know if he was really asleep or just faking it. Seeing as the man was a walking arsenal of weapons, bladed, projectile, and otherwise, he formed a rather effective barrier between Baxter and McCune.

They rolled out. Brian Gnad's truck was a former rail maintenance vehicle with *extensive* modifications. It already had rail wheels, which they could drop and ride on the rails if that was what they wanted. Brian had done all kinds of other things to it, with radio antennas, civilian and military, bar light sets to illuminate all around them, a muffler system to quiet the truck's engine noise, off-road tires and a lift kit that allowed the truck to go places that Jack could barely believe, and far more tools than he would have ever expected to fit in a garage, much less the back of the truck.

In fact, Jack would be more surprised if Brian didn't already have at least one chainsaw back there, battery-powered or otherwise. He even still had the truck-mounted flamethrower that Paul Montandon had built for him. It had worked terribly against the possessed, the undead didn't fear fire or danger and flaming undead had been far more of a hazard for his people.

Brian kept it, though, and who knew, maybe they'd need it some day?

"I hate these woods," McCune grumbled as they pulled away from the stopped train.

"Why do you say that?" Jack asked. He didn't like how hemmed in they made him feel. They limited his line of sight, like the buildings back in St. Louis.

"Too quiet," McCune grumbled.

"The woods are always quiet," Brian shrugged as he drove.

"Nah, I don't mean that. I grew up in the mountains of West Virginia," McCune snorted. "Plenty of trees, more rugged than this, too. You could go up and not see people for weeks, if ever."

He didn't speak for a long moment. "There's something *off* about these woods. They're too quiet. There's no birds. No squirrels. Nothing."

"No ghouls, either," Baxter pointed out. "No possessed. I like quiet."

"Tain't right," McCune grumbled. "Feels like the last couple places we passed are just overgrown."

"Kudzu's a thing here in Missouri, right?" Jack asked. He had noticed it, though, how the last town they passed was entirely overgrown with vines.

"Yeah, but it's not just vines, it's the trees," McCune stared out the window as the green wall went past. "There's just something *off.*"

He didn't say anything further. Jack didn't press him. He trusted the scavenger's instincts. The man had a survival knack that put most of their other survivors to shame. Plop him down in the middle of nowhere with no tools and no weapons and he would show up back at the train with a mountain of equipment and supplies.

He also managed to avoid the stuff that killed normal people.

Jack's survival skills ran a little different. He didn't avoid that kind of thing... he destroyed it.

Two miles out, they passed the markers from the last recon patrol. Seven days, ten miles per day, they hadn't been going very fast, but Jack hadn't wanted to push them too hard. They had a lot of new people, they had a whole lot of new weapons and gear, and besides, he had needed to take a little detour back to St. Louis to deal with that demonic Nighstalker thing.

"What's supposed to be ahead, anyway?" McCune asked.

"Cuba," Tom Knighton answered without opening his eyes.

"Cuba's an island, dumbass," McCune laughed.

"Cuba, Missouri, ain't," The Warrant Officer still didn't open his eyes, "call me a dumbass again and you can walk back. Scary woods or no."

McCune wisely kept his mouth shut.

The rail line and Interstate 44 both ran, more or less, parallel through the Ozark hills here. Though with the dense vegetation, they only ever seemed to see the highway when the tracks practically touched it.

"Oh, look, it's raining again," McCune said in a false tone of excitement. "Oh, and fog. This is great. Did I mention how much I love this place?"

"Shut up, McCune, no one likes the fog," Baxter snapped.

Everyone pretty much *hated* anything that limited visibility. Darkness was bad enough, though at least for that they could use lights, though those tended to draw things.

Since coming into the Ozarks, it had seemed to rain two or three times a day. Not just a light pattering, either, but, like now, a total downpour that dropped visibility to feet. And, again, as with the previous times, the heat and humidity caused a haze or fog that, even without the rain, cut the visibility still more.

"Crap, crap, crap," McCune muttered. "Why do I always get on the recon jobs with the boss? They *never* go well. I wish I had my chainsaw."

Jack ignored, him, "Can you see *anything*?"

Brian had dropped their speed to a crawl. "Not a thing."

"How long can this go on for?" Baxter asked.

"Five minutes, a week, somewhere in between?" Brian shrugged. He looked down at the mini Doppler kit that he'd installed, "There wasn't any sign of this, came out of nowhere..."

Jack felt a chill go through him at those words. Things that came out of nowhere in this hellish world, things that weren't *natural*, were dangerous. "The other truck, they stopped around here, too. Said there was some kind of rain and fog, they couldn't go on."

"Yeah..." Brian frowned. "That's why you stopped the train, right?"

"It was... now I'm wondering if maybe we shouldn't back up," Jack frowned.

"There ain't nowhere to go back the other way," McCune grumbled. "That nut-job Nidal ripped up the tracks that cross the Missouri river and go north, and we know there's no other routes across the Mississippi further back than that."

"Back in Pacific, we could have followed the Missouri river, there was that leg of track that goes that way," Jack told him.

"Why didn't we take it?" McCune muttered. "Better than this place, I wager."

"Whole lot of bridges that track runs over, and the maps show it right along the river, the river that is getting a whole lot of rain right now," Brian Gnad answered.

"Exactly that," Jack nodded. "Tracks were good the fifteen miles our people did recon over, but the river was pretty high. This much rain, the river might be even higher."

He sighed, "Push forward, Brian, let's see what we can see."

"What's Cuba look like?" McCune asked from the back seat.

"Should be a small town," Baxter offered. "Travel guide says it has about three thousand people and the world's largest rocking chair."

"Rocking chair?" Tom Knighton cracked an eye open and looked at her doubtfully.

"Forty-two feet tall," Baxter showed him a picture of it on the travel guide.

"Huh," Knighton put his head back and went back to sleep.

They drove on, a slow crawl as Brian and Jack tried to make out *anything* ahead of them. The wipers weren't even making a dent; it was as if they were under a waterfall.

The outside had gone a strange, unpleasant, greenish color. Lightning crackled, *green* lightning, that lit up the whole sky. The thunder that followed, again, almost instantly, shook the entire truck.

"I really don't like this," McCune muttered.

Jack didn't like it either. This had gone from unpleasant to terrifying.

Then, as if they had gone through a curtain, the rain cut off. The sky beyond was the same unpleasant green and wind still buffeted their truck, but the rain had cut off at least.

The wind made the trees around them seem to dance. Just ahead of them, laying across the tracks, was a fallen tree.

"Wow, is that a tree?" McCune spoke from the back seat. "If only someone had thought to bring a chainsaw, we could have made quick work of that..."

"Shut it," Jack growled. The unnaturalness with which the rain had cut off left him feeling uncertain. In the side mirror, he could see the downpour just behind them, an unnatural, unmoving wall of water. The ground here was wet, but it wasn't raining, not anymore.

"We'll need to clear that," Brian pointed out.

"I know, I know..." Jack frowned. It all felt *wrong*. Dangerous.

He didn't see any possessed or ghouls or anything. Just a tree down on the tracks and a storm behind them.

"McCune, Knighton, give me a hand," Jack told them. "Brian, you and Lieutenant Baxter stay with the truck."

"I've got the winch..." Brian offered.

"Stay with the truck," Jack ordered.

He opened the door, the wind catching it and almost ripping his shoulder out of his socket. He had to fight with it to get it closed. Then he and Warrant Officer Knighton and Sean McCune stumbled forward against the wind towards the downed tree.

It was strange, he realized, as they drew closer. The tree didn't look as if it had been toppled by the wind or blasted by that lightning. It almost looked like it had been ripped out of the ground. He could see the gnarled and twisted roots, but no hole from where they had grown.

He didn't recognize the type of tree, either. It wasn't pine or oak or anything familiar. The tree had a pebbly, almost warty, bark and thick, twisted branches. "Let's see if we can roll it off the tracks, that would be easiest."

"Yeah, easy, moving trees off the rail..." McCune shouted over the wind.

Jack stepped forward, reaching for a branch, and only as his hands touched the bark did he realize that he had made a terrible mistake.

The bark wasn't the inanimate wood that he had expected. It was warm to the touch and it pulsed under his fingers, like an animal. The branches of the trees twisted and shuddered before his eyes, one branch whipping around his torso and lifting him off his feet.

From the corner of his eye, he saw a branch punt Tom Knighton back and away, while another one caught Sean McCune as he turned to run, lifting him by one leg.

"Oh, crap," Jack shouted.

The tree that held him, rose, its trunk opening in a hideous, jagged maw.

"You know what would be great right now for fighting demonic trees?" McCune screamed. "A fucking chainsaw!"

# Chapter Two

---

Jack was about to be eaten by a tree.

He would not have guessed his day would go like this.

As the living branches of the demonic tree clenched painfully around his chest, he pawed at his harness. The branches squeezed the air right out of his lungs and his world started to narrow down.

His fingers, losing strength, found what they were looking for and he pulled the thermite grenade out of the pouch. It took him three tries to pull the pin out, his hands losing strength and the world almost black as he threw it into the gaping maw of the demon tree.

The thermite grenade ignited with a hiss, followed instantly by a shriek of hot gasses escaping.

The limbs holding him straightened and flung him away. Jack bounced, hard, against the ground and rolled, his ribs on fire as he hit.

Jack tried to sit up, but his ribs stabbed at him with agony and it was everything he could do to bite back a shriek of pain. He rolled sideways instead, the pain merely awful instead of impossible.

The demon tree, burning from the inside out, had fallen back, the long branches thrashing and scraping across the ground.

Jack feared that it would put itself out or that the fire would die on its own. Instead, its sap seemed to burn like pitch, cracking open the wood from the inside, burning hot and igniting the rest of the thing. The huge demonic tree dragged itself across the ground, towards the tree-line, leaving behind a trail of burning embers until it finally stopped moving, still burning and releasing black, tarry smoke.

Jack tried to work himself to his feet, grunted in agony and fell back.

"Knighton?" Jack croaked.

"I'm up," Knighton called. The warrant officer limped over. "You alright, sir?"

"I'm not," Jack answered, biting his lip to keep from moaning in pain. "McCune?"

"I'm great," the scavenger called. He came limping out of the woods, presumably from where the tree had flung him after Jack had thrown the thermite grenade into the thing's mouth.

The wind, still gusting, buffeted Jack as he once more tried to sit up, this time ceasing it as pain drove through his ribs. He flopped back. "I think I'm hurt."

"Shit," McCune limped over. "Like, really hurt?"

"I think it broke my ribs," Jack answered. From how his back hurt, he really hoped it hadn't broken his *back*.

He wouldn't survive that. He might not survive broken ribs, especially not if he had internal bleeding.

*Katie will be able to help.* It was a half-panicked thought, but he clung to it.

"Get me back to the truck," Jack ordered them.

"If..." McCune paused, looking at him, "Captain, if you die..."

"If I die, you know damned well what to do," Jack snapped. Anyone who died would rise up again as one of the possessed. Close to a city and all the awfulness that went on there, it might take just seconds. Out here in the wilds, it could take as long as a few hours.

"In the meantime, I'm alive, so get me back to the train." If he died, his body would rise, regardless of his injuries. The safest thing to do was to remove his limbs. From that point, they could either burn his body or just scatter the pieces.

The dead rose and walked again as possessed... or worse.

Jack couldn't help but think about the terrible *thing* that Nidal Malak had turned into, dead and yet still alive, aware... hungry.

Better that Jack's friends cut him up so that he might never hurt any of them.

The two of them lifted Jack up and he couldn't help but let out a groan of pain. They put his arms over their shoulders and walked him back to the truck. Lieutenant Baxter came out of the truck cab and the three of them helped him into the front seat. Jack felt weak and pathetic as they did it, but moving anything sent stabbing pain through his chest.

They strapped him in and he spoke without turning his head, "Back to the train."

The drive was borderline awful. Jack felt every jolt, every bump. Brian kept the speed relatively slow, but the side area of the tracks wasn't exactly a paved highway. Brian shifted them onto the rails proper and put down the rail wheels and the ride became far better.

Jack passed out a couple of times, and in between the buffeting wind, the rain, and the pain of his chest, the next thing he knew they were stopped and people were helping him out of the truck.

They used a stretcher and soon enough he was in the train car for the wounded. Katie was there, talking to him, asking him questions.

"Can you feel this?" Katie asked as she poked his foot. They had taken his boots off at some point, Jack had lost track of when.

"Yes," Jack answered.

"This?" Katie asked as she poked his thigh.

"Yeah," Jack answered her.

"What about this?" She jabbed him in the side with what felt like a red-hot poker and Jack blacked out again.

When he came to, she had leaned over his face, her expression drawn in worry, "Jack, come back to me, Jack?"

"I'm here, I didn't go anywhere," Jack mumbled at her.

"Your ribs are broken," Katie told him. "Badly broken. We don't have an X-ray; I can't look at them."

"You can wrap them, right?" Jack took shallow breaths. Breathing shallow seemed to hurt less.

"We aren't supposed to do that, not anymore," Katie answered. "You need to keep taking deep breaths."

Jack tried. It hurt.

"If you breathe shallow, you can get pneumonia," Katie told him.

"Just cracked ribs, right?" Jack spoke haltingly.

"I think they're really broken, I felt around a bit while you were out, it's... not good. If the sharp edges move around, they can puncture a lung. I don't think your back is broken. Can you wiggle your toes?"

Jack did that, weirdly, even moving just his toes pulled at muscles and made his chest hurt.

"Okay, that's good," Katie told him. "I am going to need you to lie still, don't try to sit up, don't try to do much of anything. If you *do* move around, the edges of the broken bones might slice you up inside. I don't really have the kit here to do much of anything about internal bleeding and if you slice open a lung..."

"Got it, lay here," Jack mumbled. His eyes were heavy and he wanted to assure her that everything was going to be alright. Instead, the world seemed to flow away.

***

"How is he?" Josh Wachope asked as Katie came out of the curtained area of the train car. He was a tall man, with an easy-going smile and she normally welcomed his mellow attitude.

She thought he filled in as Jack's second-in-command, though he wore Captain's rank as well.

She'd been a military doctor as a civilian for a few years, though the exact rank structure and who reported to who and why was still about as archaic to her as professional baseball statistics. *About as useful in this fallen world as well.*

She felt a churn of unease as she realized that it really mattered right now whether he was Jack's second in command or not. People would be uncertain, especially all the other new arrivals to the train. Jack had managed all of them in an easy, calm fashion... would his friend be able to do the same?

"He has badly broken ribs. I suspect he has internal bleeding, I hope he hasn't cut anything open too badly inside," Katie told him in a level voice. "He might die."

Josh's easy smile vanished. "Shit."

"Yeah, pretty much," Katie wanted to collapse and start crying. It hadn't been all that long ago that she'd had no hope, that she'd figured she would be Malak's slave doctor until he got tired of her and fed her to his master or gave her to Captain Carney.

Jack Zamora had changed that. He had rescued her, got her out. In him, she had found a partner, someone that she felt an immediate and intense connection. He gave her hope again. He destroyed Nidal Malak and his 'Hand of God'.

And now, Jack Zamora might well die.

"What can we do?" Josh Wachope asked. His eyes had gone a bit wide and his voice sounded nervous.

"He has to rest," Katie told him. "It will take weeks for his ribs to heal. Right now, if he moves around, he could puncture a lung or cause worse internal bleeding." *That's assuming he hasn't already,* she didn't say that part out loud.

She looked at him, meeting his gaze, "Until he's up and around, you're in charge." She made the decision in a split second. She didn't know if there was anyone else on the train who could do the job. In the meantime, she had to trust him to do it.

"He said that?" Josh asked uncertainly.

Katie bit her lip, "Josh, he's not exactly in a state to make any decisions."

He gave her a nod, though he looked uncertain. "I'll... I'll go tell everyone."

"Is that a good idea?" Katie asked. She worried that might cause a panic.

"They all saw us bringing him in, half of them think he's already dead. I need to calm people down," Wachope told her. He ran a hand over his face, "God, I'm not sure what I *am* going to tell them."

"That he's hurt, but he's still alive," Katie assured him. She took a deep breath, "What did this to him, some kind of undead? Is it related to the Hand of God?"

"No," Wachope assured her. "Not that we can tell, anyway. The others said that it was a tree."

"A tree fell on him?" Katie asked in surprise. That explained the broken ribs, she supposed, but she didn't see how he hadn't moved out of the way.

"No... a tree *attacked* him, McCune and Knighton told me it was like the tree was some sort of creature, McCune kept calling it a demon tree. It grabbed Jack and McCune, tossed Knighton flying, and then tried to eat the Captain."

There it was again, even Wachope called him *the Captain*. They were the same rank and Katie didn't really understand it.

She *really* didn't understand this business about a tree attacking someone. "It tried to eat him?"

"They said the trunk opened up like a sideways mouth. The Captain threw a thermite grenade inside and that burned the thing to death. I was going to lead a team out to check it out, but..."

"We need you here," Katie nodded. She covered her eyes as she considered it. "Who else can go?"

"I don't want *anyone* going out until all our patrols are back and I talk everyone through this. We've run into other bands of survivors that fell apart after their leaders died. Without leadership, people took supplies and scattered... most often we found their remains and not much else, because individuals haven't survived well on their own," Wachope shook his head. There was a tone of dread to his voice as he said that.

She remembered then that he had two young children. He and his wife lived in the same armored freight car as Katie and Jack. Was he thinking about his family right now, thinking about their survival, or that of all the train? Katie didn't know, and that worried her.

"Okay, but if this thing did that to Jack..." She frowned then. "Look, I don't know if it applies, if it's important... but I know that Nidal Malak was afraid of something out here in the woods. He wouldn't even send patrols to the edge of St. Louis on this end of town. I just sort of assumed he was scared of the trees... but now that might mean more than I thought."

Josh gave her a nod, "It might. I'll ask some of the other rescues if any of them heard anything from his people about it." He turned and then paused and looked back, "I take it that you are going to stay here?"

She gave him a nod, "I will stay with him until he gets better."

"If he..." Josh trailed off. "If he dies..."

Katie's chin came up, "If he dies, I know what we have to do."

She wasn't going to let the man she had come to love, the man who had saved her, to rise up as an undead, mindless or otherwise. She would destroy his body to prevent it. Even if it might well destroy her to do it.

"Right," Josh turned and left.

Katie turned back and went to look down at Jack. She gently rested her hand on his forehead, reassured by the beat of his pulse at his temple and the movement of his chest. *You cannot die,* she silently told him, *we need you. I need you.*

# Chapter Three

"THAT'S THE LAST OF them," James Ott told Josh Wachope as a recon crew piled out of their truck and came up to the group. Two of them were supporting a third, the man swearing as he limped up. James, a former State Trooper, led a recon team of several other former-law enforcement personnel.

"You were attacked?" Josh asked. He'd been Jack's number two for so long that he knew what he needed to do, yet he felt off-balance. His friend had been in charge for so long, had thrown himself at anything and everything head-on and emerged. This was the first time he hadn't... and in this world, even the slightest injury could be the end. *And that wasn't a slight injury, he might well die...*

"It was the damndest thing, sir," James told him as the three came up. "We was stopped on the road, trying to figure out a way around some downed trees. These vines, they crawled right up Tony's legs, started pulling him towards the trees. It was like they were alive."

*Shit.* "The Captain got attacked by a tree. Something's going on," Josh had never thought he might say words like that. It sounded absurd. Plants didn't *move*, much less attack anyone.

Josh shook himself, "You hurt?"

Tony Dutson raised his pant legs. Welts and bruises rose up his legs to his knees, and the skin had started to blister. "It burns like poison ivy; those things squeezed me so hard I lost feeling in my legs. I don't want to think about what would have happened if they hadn't cut me free."

"Alright, go see the doc," Josh told him. "This happened up north?"

"We had just got to the RV park on the map, it's completely overgrown, trees down over the road, partially flooded and..." James Ott trailed off, as if he didn't really believe the words he was about to say.

"Carnivorous vines, I got it," Josh gave them a nod. "Get him some help."

Josh walked towards the next group, "Gomez, how did things look down south?"

They were still sending scouting teams out to look for supplies and survivors, though with how two of those teams had been attacked, Josh was starting to rethink that. Gomez's team had gone south from Leasburg. Gomez wasn't military, he had run a landscaping business in Ohio, he and his immediate family had met up with the train there, and he'd been running his former landscaping truck as a recon truck in the time since.

"We didn't get very far, lots of trees down and roads washed out a couple of places," Gomez answered.

"Any... uh, issues with those trees?" Josh asked.

"Nah, just too big to try and move, most of them," Gomez frowned, clearly puzzled by the question.

"Any weird plants or vines?" Josh asked. He felt a little crazy as he asked it. Plants didn't come to life and attack people. *Yeah, and the dead don't rise and murder the living, but here we are...*

"Everything's overgrown, I mean, we saw Leasburg when we went through, but it gets worse the further south you go," Gomez answered. "I mean, there's trees growing out of houses that I wouldn't say could have grown so quickly. You sure couldn't pay me enough to try and trim this shit back. It's eerie."

"Any survivors?" Josh asked. He knew the answer, Gomez would have brought that up first.

The man spat, "I didn't even see any possessed, much less any survivors. Whole forest was dead quiet." He muttered something in Spanish and made the sign of the cross. "To be honest, it was worse than the city in some ways. When I told my crew we were turning back, no one complained."

"Gracias," Josh gave him a nod. "We're not sending any more patrols out for a bit. Get yourself something to eat and get some rest. We'll have a group meeting here soon."

He moved on, checking in with others and spreading the word in person that they'd have a meeting. Most of the military survivors and what he considered para-military, which included cops, firefighters, and the like, were sanguine about it.

The civilians asked questions. Half of them wanted to know whether the Captain was alright. The other half had ideas, suggestions, some of them helpful, many of them half-baked or completely illogical. They had so many new people, rescues from St. Louis that had all kinds of thoughts and ideas and who weren't part of their original crew.

Josh managed to smile and nod to them, though inside he was trying hard not to snap at them. He didn't *want* to be in charge. He had been perfectly happy to leave that to Jack, and for good reason. Leading a military team, going into combat, that was why he had joined the Army. That he understood, and he understood how to lead and command them without hesitation.

Being in charge of over a thousand mixed military and civilians was *not* something he understood or even wanted to do. Jack had handled the civilians with patience and one-on-one, handling them with an ease that Josh had envied a bit.

Josh had been Special Forces; he knew how to build teams and organize people to meet a threat. He knew how to train civilians to fight, in conventional and unconventional methods. What he could admit to himself, though, was that he didn't have the same focus and driving goal that Jack brought to it. Josh could direct and lead, he couldn't *inspire* them. He wasn't their *Captain*, not like Jack.

With Jack healthy, that wasn't a problem. Josh could coach and mentor, cajole and occasionally bully, and get people to do what they needed to do to stay alive. People looked to their leader and viewed Josh as the muscle.

Only now, Jack was hurt, maybe even dying, and they were looking to *him* to lead.

Soon enough, everyone had gathered around the front of the train, all but those on guard duty. The sun had started to dip. They weren't going to light fires, as the light would draw possessed, not that they had seen any really since St. Louis. *Maybe that is what we should have taken as a sign.*

Josh climbed up on the front of the train where they all could see him. "So," he began, "for those of you who haven't heard, Captain Zamora was hurt today."

They started muttering and talking back and forth. He went on, because he wanted to head off any kind of panic, "Doc Katie says he's going to be down for a few weeks or so..."

"Who's in charge?" A man shouted from the back.

"...and he left me in charge," Josh finished.

"Why's the military got to be in charge?" A woman asked from the front. She was a small woman, one of the new people, someone he didn't recognize.

Before Josh could appropriately answer that, another person spoke up, "Maybe it's a sign, maybe we should turn back."

"I heard he got attacked by a tree, that doesn't make any sense," This came from Luis Cedano. "Trees don't attack people." The Professor seemed particularly irritated by the very idea.

"He was attacked by something that looked like a tree," Josh told them. "We don't know exactly what it was... and Tony Dutson got attacked by some kind of living vine."

"He's got blisters where it touched him," James Ott spoke up, "like poison ivy."

"Plants don't attack people!" The heckler from the back called.

"And the dead don't rise up and attack the living, and blood doesn't rain from the sky, and demonic monsters don't suck the souls out of people," Josh snapped. The group went quiet at the anger in his tone. "Look, people, we live in a pretty horrible world, we seem to have found someplace where plants *do* attack people."

The group went quiet and eyes went to the trees around them, the still forest where no birds sang and no animals moved.

Josh could feel the group draw closer to one another, like a herd of animals sensing a predator watching them.

*If they're too afraid to argue, maybe that'll be a good thing.*

As if to disprove that theory, one of them shouted, "We should turn south, the track goes south at Cuba."

Robert Brockman spoke up, "Yeah, uh, that section of track doesn't go anywhere, it leads up to a mining area and terminates." He didn't say it loud, though, and Josh could tell about half the crowd didn't hear his words.

"South is better than this, we should get to Texas, we heard their transmissions, they're holding out in towns down there," The woman at the front stated. There was a level of confidence and self-assurance to her words that bothered Josh.

"We are already headed southwest," Josh told them all. They were going more south than he really wanted. "That track that turns straight south will end long before we get out of the hills and woods, much less anywhere near Texas."

The woman spoke again, "We can find trucks or maybe just split up," Those words were exactly what Josh hadn't wanted to hear from any of the survivors. "Maybe that would be best."

"Can't we just backtrack to the other tracks, the ones that went west?" Luis Cedano asked.

"There's a lot of rain, in case you didn't notice," Josh spoke in a tight tone. "There are a lot of washouts, we're worried the Missouri river is over the banks and the tracks may not go through, this route has more hills, but less bridges and rivers to worry about."

21

"Why do we even need the train?" The woman at the front asked. "We have all the military trucks and service trucks." The way she pitched her voice, she was talking to the crowd more than him and it set his back up.

"We can't move everyone and all the supplies we need via trucks," Josh felt like he had lost control, and before he had even finished another person asked a question, then another.

"Let's put it to a vote," the heckler from the back called.

"Yeah, that's the fair thing to do, vote on it," the woman at the front nodded. Her tone sounded far to assured for his liking.

"What if you don't like the way the vote goes?" Robert Brockman asked.

"Then we can just go our own separate ways," Someone from the crowd called. "There's no need for us to stick together, I mean, we did fine on our own before."

"Was that before or after Nidal Malak had captured you and turned you into his plantation slaves?" Josh snapped.

The man he'd called out scowled at his reminder and the crowd quieted a bit.

"We need to stick together," Josh told them. "There are *things* out there that, if we split up, they will hunt us down individually or in small groups. Sticking together gives us all a better chance."

"I don't see why you get to make this decision for the rest of us," the woman protested.

"Let's see where we *can* go before we argue about it," Josh snapped. She didn't look happy at that and half the crowd got to muttering.

"Look," Josh growled, "I'm in charge. The Captain put me in charge. Until he's back on his feet —"

"What if he dies?" The heckler from the back asked.

The whole group went silent at that.

"He won't," Josh told them.

"What if he *does*," the woman at the front asked and Josh could swear he saw her smile as she said it. *She knows she's stirring them up, getting them afraid.* He had to fight an impulse to have someone grab her, figure out who she was and why she was causing problems. If he did that now, it might cause a riot with how on-edge everyone had become.

Josh looked around at all of them. There was fear, worry, and he saw plenty of insubordination and resistance as well. They didn't like him in charge. Maybe Jack could have kept them on track, or maybe this unease had been boiling away since St. Louis. *There are too many of them who are new to this, who hate living on the train, who think they can do better.*

"If it comes to that, we'll put it to a vote," Josh told them. He was lying as he said it, though. There was no way he'd trust the life of his family to this lot or a vote.

He had seen too many survivors do stupid things because that was what they decided to do as a group. In Josh's opinion, a group of people working together to come up with a decision most often went to the level of the lowest intelligence individual of the group, if not lower.

*Jack will pull through, and I'll keep this lot together until then.*

He wondered if he was lying to himself.

\*\*\*

Meelah felt a tingle of excitement as the group broke away. She never would have expected things to go so perfectly wrong so soon after joining the train's survivors.

She had hoped, initially, to find her way into their leader's good graces. She had done much the same with Nidal Malik, after all, talking her way first into his company and then into his bed. Sure, with him, she had been one of several women he enjoyed.

Still, she had earned his protection, and even the mark of his God, in the form of a tattoo on her chest, right between her breasts. He had talked to her, too, about leading, about power, and she had learned everything she could. It hadn't been hard to pretend to fawn over how smart he was and let him talk about all his plans, all the details of how he stayed in charge.

In her experience, powerful men liked to talk about themselves, liked to feel important. Nidal had been no exception. She had figured this Captain Jack who ran the train would be the same, but it seemed that he already had one woman and since that was the Doctor that Nidal had captured, Meelah hadn't wanted to risk the woman recognizing her and she had avoided them both.

She especially hadn't wanted anyone with any authority to recognize her, not with the terrible things Meelah had done to earn her tattoo and her place with Nidal. There had been the ceremony, where she and other survivors had to sacrifice one of their own, one chosen by Nidal, and they had then been introduced to the Hand of God to receive his blessing.

Meelah's chest burned as she thought of it and a chill settled through her so that she shivered, despite the summer warmth. She had done what she had to do to survive, to thrive. She did not regret the screaming woman that she had sacrificed, for she knew that the others would have sacrificed her just as readily had she been selected instead.

Here at the train, Meelah had turned her attentions to winning over others on the train in the days since the fall of her former master. That hadn't been hard. Several of Nidal's junior people had slipped aboard with the other escapees. She'd sought them out and won over a few of the other survivors, too. And they had taken the opportunity during the frequent stops along the train's slow progress to talk and work out the beginnings of a plan.

*Her* plan, of course.

"What do you think?" Meelah asked as she moved up next to Marrik.

"I don't know," He spoke in a harsh rasp, a product of the scar that ran across his neck.

She liked that scar, it made people shy away from him, made them wary and afraid of him. He used that, too, to scare those who recognized him from when he worked with Nidal.

"We could move now," Marrik offered.

Meelah scowled, "Not a chance. If we tried to take over, the Army types would gun us down."

They had a few weapons. But there were more people loyal to the Captain. There wasn't enough confusion and worry, either. "I'll talk with Fuller and some of the others."

"I don't trust Fuller," Marrik rasped.

Neither did she. He led one of the recon teams and he had been with the train for months. But he wasn't trusted by the train's folk, not entirely, either. He had more of the look and act of a raider than one of the train folk. She didn't care about that, not right now.

"I'll have Shamika talk to him," Meelah reassured him. "She says he thinks with his prick."

"She thinks every man thinks with his prick," Marrik rasped.

Meelah gave him a look and he actually flushed and looked away. She knew *he* had slept with Shamika, after all. The woman hopped from bed to bed, based off whatever relative worth she saw in such arrangements. Her *assets* gave her an advantage there, not that Meelah wasn't her match in looks, at least.

Shamika had also had her tubes tied, so she didn't care about risk of pregnancy. Meelah envied her that, as she'd seen too many women die in childbirth in the months after the collapse.

"I'll work some of our other friends," Meelah murmured. "You... see if you can stir up some fear. Get people worried, frightened people make all kinds of stupid decisions."

Marrik smiled at that. He liked to scare people, especially those weaker than him.

"We'll take the train," Meelah assured him. "From there, we'll set ourselves up as rulers."

Marrik probably saw himself as a king. That was fine, Meelah didn't have to be the leader, she just wanted all the perks, and she knew that Marrik was easy enough to manipulate and direct, just as she did now.

Just as she would the rest of the people on the train.

Even as she thought that, the tattoo between her breasts seemed to burn for just a moment, a flare that was there and gone before the even consciously realized it.

# Chapter Four

"SOMETHING IS COMING," THE voice spoke from the echoing depths of the cave.

The Priestess shuddered as that voice trembled through her. She felt it in her bones, the words making her flesh tremble. She fell to her knees, "What should I do, oh mistress?" On the steel and concrete platform, she felt warmth flow through her as she answered the call.

This was her goddess, after all, and that she chose to speak to her at any time was a wonder.

"It has killed one of the Keepers," her lady spoke, "killed her with fire."

The Priestess shuddered again, though this time not in religious ecstasy, but in fear. The Kin and the Keepers were mighty, and her Mistress was powerful, but they rightfully feared fire. It was a tool of destruction, a weapon of unmaking and chaos.

Her mistress brought order, brought life, and creation. Her Kin and her Keepers kept away those that would threaten the Priestess and her people. That protection came at a cost, of course, but such things often required sacrifices. There was no life without death.

"Find out more, find out who has sent it," The powerful voice of her mistress spoke from deep inside the cave, from the massive underground lake below her. The Priestess's eyes could make out the water shifting, her Mistress's bulk stirring the waters.

Even though she loved and worshipped her goddess, she did not dare to even think of swimming in those waters. She had seen what happened to those sent below. She honored the price that her Mistress demanded. That did not mean she wanted to be one of them.

"And then, oh great one?" The Priestess asked. She fully expected what the answer would be, though she knew what would be coming.

"Destroy them."

***

"Half these idiots want to scatter in all directions," Josh growled. "The other half don't want to move anywhere at all."

"They're afraid," Robert Brockman told him. The architect adjusted his glasses, "I mean, they have good reasons."

Josh shot a dubious look at him. He knew that Brockman and Jack were long-time friends and he appreciated the man's knowledge. That didn't mean he always agreed with what he had to say.

"Look, we have two people attacked by *plants*," Brockman pointed out. "One of them the Captain... and we are surrounded by trees."

"Mark Twain National Forest is just south of here," Tim Kennedy pointed out. The big man had a background in logistics and he managed both their internal logistics and referenced train depots and picked out likely spots for resupply. That had been their main source, finding abandoned trains parked along sections of track, where they'd been able to get fuel and food.

Josh was feeling a bit outnumbered in the engine cab. Normally this served as what Josh thought of as their command post, with Brockman's computer, Tim's maps, and all the copious notes they had. The chalk board with the running count of survivors as well: 1808.

Normally Jack ran these meetings or, if he was out, Josh would sort of chair them. But Jack was injured and Josh felt out of his depth.

"If those civilians out there split up or scatter, half of them will be dead within a week," Josh pointed out. "And we *can't* stay here, this isn't exactly a defensible spot and the whole point of the train is that it *moves*."

"Uh, don't forget, we're both civilians," Brockman pointed out and Kennedy snorted at that.

"How could I?" Josh growled. He shook himself, then, "Look, sorry, I'm just trying to keep everything together. Alright, what are our real options?"

"Maybe we should turn back?" Brockman suggested. "We don't know for sure that the track is down over the Missouri river. We were headed west anyway, that line of tracks goes to Kansas City and then straight out west, right?"

Tim gave a nod, though he was looking at Josh as if he weren't sure what to think. "Yeah. But the scouts said the river was *really* high and there are some stretches of that track that ran right along the bank. If the river jumped the bank, the track might just be gone. Not to mention the bridges."

"Our best bet is to keep on towards Springfield, Missouri," Josh nodded.

"Not turn south at Cuba?" Brockman asked.

"Definitely not," Tim and Josh both answered.

"Go ahead," Josh waved at him.

"Thanks," Tim nodded, "Look, that route goes to... uh, south, right into Mark Twain National Forest, and it dead-ends at a town called..."

"Viburnum," Brockman nodded, "I know, but..."

"There's nothing down there. The town is barely a spot on the map and it's in the middle of the woods," Tim scoffed.

"I mean, there *might* be survivors, towns like that are tough, they're remote enough scavengers and possessed don't typically threaten them and they're full of tough people who work hard," Josh felt the need to point out. "Still, if they are survivors, they aren't going to exactly welcome a thousand more people. And there's nowhere to go from there."

He didn't state the obvious, either, that if there were some carnivorous plants in the area, the dense Mark Twain National Forest probably wasn't a good place to go into to avoid them.

"Look," Josh went on, "We've got a couple more towns on the way, and then we hit Springfield. If we can scout it out, we can probably make it there in a single day of travel."

"What about the switch over to Fort Leonard Wood?" Tim asked.

Josh considered that. "Have we heard anything on the radio?"

"Not a thing," Brockman shook his head. "Not on the shortwave, not on the military radios."

"We're still probably a bit far out for the military radios to pick up, especially with the hills," Josh shrugged, "but honestly, if there were any survivors there, you would think we would see some indicators." Fort Leonard Wood was the home of US Army Engineers, Military Police, and Chemical Soldiers, it had a huge basic training and advanced training complex and a variety of military schools, but it wasn't exactly fortified.

It was remote, though. And the advantage it might have there was the same that many of the small towns that had held out had: being remote and with a small enough population that the undead or predatory survivors didn't overwhelm it.

The towns along the interstate could have fallen to scavengers or possessed from St. Louis. *Or evil plants,* Josh reminded himself, even as he considered the ridiculousness of the thought.

"We need to push forward," Josh told them both.

"What about the ones wanting to vote?" Brockman asked

"I don't *care* what they want," Josh snapped. "If we put this to a vote, half of them will vote for whatever harebrained idea someone else comes up with and we'll all likely end up dead."

"If you just tell everyone what to do, some people might get really upset," Brockman suggested.

30

"Then they can deal with it and still be alive," Josh scowled. He took a deep breath, "I'll call the scouts together, we'll push the scouts forward and as soon as we're clear to move, we'll roll out."

"What about if you run into more killer trees?" Tim asked.

"Then we kill them," Josh answered.

*Or they kill us.* It was pretty much the way things went.

***

Captain Jack Zamora woke up his chest aching and his head feeling feverish. The very first thing he tried to do was sit up and as pain drove into him, he hissed and lay back.

"Jack?" He heard Katie's voice and he turned his head.

"What's happening?" Jack asked. He managed to avoid trying to turn his head once more.

"You need to lie still, as much as possible," Katie told him.

"I got that," Jack said dryly. He realized what had bothered him. There was no sound of movement, there wasn't really much sound at all. The train's engine wasn't running. They were stopped. They needed to keep moving.

"Why aren't we moving?" Jack asked. His head felt foggy as he asked it, and he had to fight a moment of panic as he thought about Nidal Malak and the Hand of God. They had dealt with both of them, right? That hadn't just been a dream... or a nightmare?

"Captain Wachope has sent out scouts ahead," Katie told him. There was a tone of disapproval to her voice as she said it.

"What's wrong?" Jack asked.

"Some people want to turn back, to try another way, some people want to turn south," Katie told him.

"We have to go on," Jack mumbled. It felt like to much effort to force the words out and even as he said them, his eyelids felt heavy. What was wrong with him? Why couldn't he stay awake?

"We will, Jack, just rest, okay?" Katie assured him.

He didn't really hear her. He sank back into unconsciousness.

***

"Do you have to go?" Howie asked. He was Sandra's youngest child. Sean McCune had taken a liking to the boy, really to the widow's entire family, though he felt uneasy to say any such thing to them.

Feelings, that wasn't what a man talked about, not in Sean's opinion.

"Yeah, kid," Sean told him. His whole leg hurt and he had to mask a limp as he shouldered his pack, this time with an electric chainsaw strapped to the outside. "It'll be fine."

"Mom said the Captain was hurt, hurt bad, maybe like my..." The boy didn't finish, his face wrinkling up in worry and sorrow. Sean knew he was thinking about his father, who the Lord Protector had killed and brought back as one of the possessed.

Sean knelt meeting the boy's eyes. "Look. The Captain's tough, tougher than anyone I know, he'll be fine."

"What about you?" Howie asked. Behind him, Sean saw the boy's mother standing there, watching him.

Sean forced himself to smile, "I may not be as tough as the Captain, but I'm twice as slippery. I'll skate out of any trouble and be back here before you know it. Now, remember what I told you before, about being brave for your mother?"

Howie nodded.

"Alright, then, I gotta go. Uncle Larry is waiting," Sean had taken to calling his friend that in front of Sandra's kids. He didn't know why. It sort of seemed like the thing to call him.

32

He straightened, his leg throbbing at him. He had welts around his calf where the demon tree had grabbed him, and just like Tony's skin, his had blistered from contact with the thing. He ignored the pain as he stepped over to Sandra. "You'll be fine," he assured her.

"What about you?" She asked in a faint voice.

Sean gave her the same confident smirk he knew worked swell. "Like I told Howie, I'll be back before you know it."

He didn't pull her in for a kiss or anything like that. He just reached out a hand and took hers and gave it a squeeze. Sean could admit that for other women, he would have kissed and maybe more, but that didn't seem right with Sandra. She wasn't some floozy who he wanted roll with; she was a decent woman. Probably the only decent woman who would as much as give him the time of day.

Sean gave her hand one last squeeze and then he turned away, jumping out of the train car and only realizing as his leg went out from under him that that had been a terrible idea.

"I got you," Larry Southard told him, catching him by the shoulder and preventing him from falling. "Damn, Sean, you go off on a mission or two with the Captain and you lose all your balance."

"Thanks, Larry," Sean told him. He squinted at his long-time friend. Between the pair of them, they tended to find the best loot for their band of survivors. Sean could admit that a lot of that skill came from living on the *questionable* side of the law for most of his life. He'd been in and out of jail, more often than he would want to admit.

He had never asked Larry what he did before all this, and Larry had given him the same courtesy.

"I'm surprised you volunteered for this," Sean admitted.

Larry chortled, "Oh, buddy, did you hear about the town up ahead?"

"Cuba, Missouri?" Sean asked doubtfully. "World's biggest rocking chair?"

"*Past* Cuba, and I'm not talking about a rocking chair," Larry leaned in, his eyes excited.

"What do you mean?" Sean asked. He hadn't really looked at the maps. Anything more than a few hours away really didn't exist for him.

"Place called *Rolla*, buddy," Larry grinned. "It's a *mining* town."

"Mining?" Sean asked as they walked towards the truck.

"Yeah, like *gold* mining," Larry slapped him on the shoulder.

"Gold?" Sean considered that, shooting his friend a dubious look. Granted, there was still some trade value in jewelry and gold and silver. Not as much, as things like bullets, booze, and birth control, in his opinion.

"Gold. They've got a mining museum, seems like the kind of place to look into, right?" Larry asked him. He pulled out a much-folded brochure, the kind of thing that they'd find at truck stops and abandoned hotels along their route, the kind of thing that often enough served as clues for where they might find things of value.

Sean hadn't really cared much for museums. He looked at the brochure with a frown, until Larry's fingers pointed to a display... with a lot more gold than he had ever seen anywhere in his life.

Sure, there wasn't anyone here and now who might want it, but they were headed out west. There would be people who might want it... and gold was... well it was *gold*.

Sean got a gleam to his eye and he looked over at his friend. "Yeah, that might... that might be something we need to check out. There could be, uh, mining tools and stuff, right?"

"Yeah, mining tools," Larry slapped him on the shoulder. "We're going to be rich."

Sean thought about Sandra and her kids, and how they worried about him. He thought about the gold and wondered if it was worth risking his life, risking what he'd got.

*Maybe that gold will help me buy them some security, some safety,* he told himself.

"Yeah, rich," Sean told his friend.

***

Sergeant Ronald Shaw, United States Army, restrained a groan as he saw McCune and his pal Southard come walking up. He hadn't had to work with either of the pair, not since the Captain had rescued him and the survivors he'd been leading from a federal prison that they had been holed up in.

That said, he had heard a lot about the two of them and the trouble they tended to find.

"How are we looking?" Shaw asked of Brian Gnad.

"Not bad, truck's fine, there's a storm a few miles out, but just the usual for here," Brian told him, looking over at him. "Why?"

"Just... nervous," Shaw admitted. The Captain had gone this way and he'd come back barely alive. They'd said a *tree* attacked him.

Captain Wachope had selected Shaw to lead the next scouting mission. Shaw had been stationed here; he'd been down at Fort Leonard Wood for almost five years. Shaw wasn't a cavalry scout or Marine Recon or anything like that, though. He was a cook. Sure, he'd survived and led a group of civilians to safety in the federal prison back at Jacksonville, Illinois, but he wasn't exactly a natural born hero like the Captain.

He was tall and black; he wore the same ragged uniform he'd worn since his convoy had been bogged down by possessed near Chicago and he and the other survivors had scattered to find help.

He wasn't an experienced member of the Captain's team. He would have thought they'd select Sergeant Pape for the assignment, or maybe that Captain Wachope would lead the mission himself.

For that matter, Lieutenant Baxter already sat in the truck. And Warrant Officer Knighton had been on the mission, too, though Captain Wachope had ordered the walking armory to stay here at the train rather than come on this mission.

Shaw had seen the man head to the train's machine shop, though what he was doing, he had no idea.

Lieutenant Baxter, well didn't really act like an officer most of the time. She just worked the radios and kept to herself. She hadn't even blinked when Captain Wachope had put Shaw in charge, as an NCO, over her as an officer.

Brian Gnad's much-upgraded truck had a slew of radios, as well, though Shaw knew that if they saw any signs of survivors or wanted to keep concealed, they'd leave him and his truck and continue on foot.

Larry Southard and Sean McCune made the rest of his scouting team. They were going to go right down the tracks while two more trucks went along the winding Route 66 and Interstate 44 that paralleled, more or less, the railroad tracks. Sergeant Pape had the winding Route 66 while Fuller and his crew were on the interstate. It gave Shaw a bit of comfort knowing there were two other trucks headed out with them, though one of them being Fuller didn't make him feel as good about it.

Shaw climbed in up font while Larry and Sean piled in the back seat with Lieutenant Baxter.

"Everyone good?" Shaw asked, feeling a bit overwhelmed.

"Let's roll," Larry gave him thumbs up.

Shaw just gave him a nod, swallowing a bit as he looked in the side-mirror back at the train. He had to fight a moment of welling panic. What if something happened while they were gone? What if they couldn't get back?

He buried that sensation of panic and just gave Brian Gnad a nod. "Let's roll."

# Chapter Five

"CAN YOU BELIEVE THIS shit?" Sergeant Tyler Pape growled as they drove down the road.

"What?" Julie Frost asked. She'd been on a bird photography trip on the East Coast when the world had fallen apart. The woman had a single digital camera in a pouch that had proven useful enough that the Captain had authorized her to charge its batteries regularly. She was also one of the quietest, stealthiest people Tyler had ever met, and there were stories of her slipping out ahead on foot and managing to slip through brush, trees, and wilderness without a sound.

Sergeant Pape had worked with the scout before, though most often Pape ended up on train guard detail. Pape wasn't exactly a stealthy guy. He was *big* for one thing, with a mass of bone and muscle that gave him a natural advantage when it came to fending off possessed from trying to climb onto their train.

"Trees, everywhere," Pape growled. "I *hate* the trees."

She gave a laugh, "Yeah, trees and hills, that's the Ozarks, man." She shot him a look, "You haven't been here, before?"

"I had... I was doing a cross-country motorcycle ride... came around a bend on this highway almost six years ago." Sergeant Pape's gaze went out the windows, his eyes upon the trees. The rain that they'd been expecting had come in and the eerie fog had begun to rise as well.

"Rainy day, came around a bend and some jackass was driving down the middle of the road. He clipped me, sent me into the ditch," Sergeant Pape shuddered a bit at the memory. "I lay there for four hours before someone saw my bike and called someone. Spent three months in the hospital, I've got eight titanium screws in my pelvis thanks to the damned trees out here."

"Sorry to hear that," Julie shot him a look. "I'm surprised you don't walk with a limp."

"I worked hard at it. I ended up missing a deployment, my best friends all went," Tyler looked back at her. "They took an IED a week into that deployment, while I was lying in a hospital trying to learn how to walk again. They all died."

It had driven him to work hard, to get back on his feet, to fight to stay in the Army.

And here he was, still alive after most of the world had died.

"Sean McCune said it was a tree that attacked the Captain," Julie noted.

"McCune says a lot of things," Pape snapped. He was still raw over the reminder of the loss of his friends.

"Well..." She trailed off as they came around a bend, slowing their truck to a halt.

There was a wreck, at least, it looked like that was what had happened. There were five or six cars piled up in the road, with a larger truck sideways across the road as well. Vines had overgrown the lot of it, thick with leaves and making it hard to even see past. There wasn't a lot of room to get their truck through, on the one side was a ditch, on the other, saplings had grown up right up to the shoulder of the road.

"I don't like this," Sergeant Pape growled. He looked at the back seat, where the rest of their scout team waited. "Martins, Stein, out to the left, Meehan, right with me."

He looked at Julie, "Back the truck up to the bend, radio the train, let them know there's some kind of barricade here."

They hadn't even gotten to the area where the road and rail met up again. This was out in the middle of nowhere.

Tyler rolled out of the truck and shut the door, carrying his rifle at the low-ready as he and Meehan went to the right. He didn't move into the trees, though the space between his shoulder blades itched and he couldn't fight the feeling that they were being watched.

He waved at Meehan, the former state trooper dropping back a bit. If this was an ambush, Sergeant Pape didn't want the pair of them in the kill zone.

The vines growing over the vehicles seemed far too heavy to just be a few months old. For that matter, the vehicles had a rusted, abandoned look, as if they had been here, rotting away in the rain for decades.

Martins and Stein had made it up on the left.

"See anything?" Sergeant Pape asked in a low voice.

"No movement," Martins answered. "You, sergeant?"

"Negative," Pape told them. The ditch was deep on this side, and the rain had water in it flowing fast. That seemed like a good way to lose his footing and take a fall.

He reached out, catching hold of one of the thick vines on the cars and started to ease around the edge of the ditch on this side.

Of course, that was when the vine he held moved under his gloved fingers and a braid of vine crawled up his arm to his elbow and started to pull him in.

Sergeant Pape let out a squawk of surprise, just as the entire *mass* of vines shuddered and more vines spread out, moving with startling speed. Another pair of them ensnared his feet at the ankles, even as the one holding his left arm started to pull him in.

Sergeant Pape let go his rifle, the friction cord dropping it to his chest. He shouted a warning even as he drew his K-bar, going to the knife with the survival instincts drilled into him from fighting the undead that could appear at any moment without warning.

The first thing he did was bring the knife down on the vine on his wrist, sawing at it even as he heard his people shouting in alarm as the vines went after them, too.

Tough or not, his big knife cut through the vine holding his wrist. Unfortunately for him, that had been holding him tight against the wrecks and he fell back as the vines holding his feet started to pull him in from the bottom.

Sergeant Pape knew if those vines dragged him up under the wrecks, he was as good as dead.

He sat up, knife slashing and hacking at the vines that held his feet and that dragged him half-under the wreck of a car. He managed to get one foot free and sawed at a vine thicker than his wrist that had gone all the way up his leg to his hip.

This one whipped at him, catching him across the side of the head and dazing him for a moment. When he came back to himself, he was pulled up under the car up to his chest and he had to kick and pull to get back out enough to swing his knife again. This time his blade cut into the thickest vine, hot, black sap spattering across him as he sliced through and then dragged himself away from the wrecks.

Off to the side, he saw Martins and Stein in a tug-of-war with a mass of vines, a dozen or more vines wrapping Martins to the point that the Marine looked almost like a mummy.

Sergeant Pape rushed over, knife swinging, joined a moment later by Meehan who hacked down into the thicker vines with his machete, even while Sergeant Pape used his knife to cut individual vines and Stein pulled Martins back.

The vines let go and they all stumbled away. They were covered in sticky sap and pieces of twitching vines and Sergeant Tyler Pape felt more than a little crazy as he backed away from the mass of hostile vegetation.

"What the hell was that, Sergeant?" Martins panted, even as he tried to pull wrapped vines off himself, his hands trembling.

"I don't know and —"

Words failed him as the entire wreck site shuddered and moved. A vine as thick around as a fire hose shoved a vehicle wreck to the side. Bones, human and animal, spilled out from underneath the wreck. Little red vines, crawling over the bones like tentacles, pawed at the air. A heavy bulk, as big around as a small sedan, rose up, thick vines as big around that, as Tyler's leg, moved and flexed, lifting the huge, carnivorous plant from its lair.

"Fucking shoot it," Tyler shouted.

They opened fire. Against a mass of possessed they would have used single shots, blowing out leg joints or something to slow them. Against this horrifying *thing*, they fired indiscriminately into it. Tyler emptied his magazine into it, seeing leaves and bits of it explode out. The vine monster didn't scream or make any noise at all, though it drew back, thick vines positioned in front of its body as bullets ripped into it. It eased over behind the wrecked truck, dragging its vines with it even as Tyler Pape pawed to reload.

The trailing vines went with the thing, until there was nothing left in the road besides a pile of bones and the wrecked cars.

"Did we..." Sergeant Pape looked over at his team, "Did that shit just happen?"

***

"Rain, vines, trees, more rain, more vines, more trees," Larry muttered in the back seat.

"Can you please shut up?" Sergeant Shaw asked.

On the radio, he'd been listening to Julie Frost squawk something about being under attack. She'd finished up reporting some kind of plant that had attacked, though it didn't make a whole lot of sense to Shaw.

They hadn't seen anything like that. The rain had grown extremely heavy, though it had eased up a bit. Brian Gnad had muttered a bit as they came out of the worst of it, though Shaw was just glad that they had *some* visibility.

"It sounds like they're alright," Lieutenant Baxter said after a moment. "Though they're headed back to the train."

Sergeant Shaw considered that, not thrilled by that. True, they couldn't exactly take the train down that road, but it was nice to have someone else out here with them. The third scout truck had gone up towards the interstate and it would be a good while until the railroad tracks and the interstate met up again. Route 66 and the train tracks had already joined up, so if Sergeant Pape had continued on, he would have linked up with them.

They were going past some kind of abandoned and overgrown parking area and a heavily overgrown sign advertised "The Best Ozark Lumber."

Ahead of them, the trees thick to either side, emerging out of the rain and fog, Sergeant Shaw could make out buildings.

"I think this is where we ran into that... tree thing," Brian said as he slowed. "It's kind of hard to tell."

"Yeah, it was over there," Sean pointed at a spot that looked pretty much the same to Shaw as everything else around here.

"I don't see anything there, now," Shaw couldn't fight the feeling that this was some kind of elaborate prank, even though he had seen them bring back the Captain all beat up.

"Just some scorch marks," Lieutenant Baxter said in a quiet voice. "The thing burned until there was nothing left, see?"

Brian Gnad crept his truck past the spot and Shaw could barely make out a blackened area of rock and grass.

They continued on, pulling past overgrown homes and a gas station that had good-sized trees growing up through the windows.

"Any sign of survivors?" Shaw asked, though he didn't for a moment think they would see anyone. The whole town had a dead, abandoned feel to it. It wasn't anything he could describe, it was something he knew the feel of, though, living in a dying world.

"There's no bodies, no dancing fruit," Sean said in a low voice. Normally, in almost every town they'd been through, they saw 'dancing fruit' of people who had been trapped in high places, watching their supplies dwindle, and rather than starving to death or worse, they'd hung themselves, only for their bodies to come back as undead, to dance and spin in their nooses, mindlessly trying to get free and serving as morbid notices that there were no living survivors to find.

They crept through the dead town. Almost every building was overgrown with vines, saplings, even small trees. Grass, some of it as tall as the truck, grew up in the medians of the roads and in front of houses. Roots had split the road in a couple of spots and saplings were starting to grow up in the road itself.

They stopped at the track junction. Sergeant Shaw jumped out to check it, though the switch was set for the main fork that they wanted and everything looked good. Even standing there, he fought the eerie feeling of being watched by something hostile.

The rock on the tracks had some vines growing up it, and grass as well, but not enough to impede their advance through the town. "Should we check out anything in town?" Larry asked from the back seat. He didn't sound all that enthusiastic.

"We're good on supplies and I don't see anything that looks promising... do you?" Sergeant Shaw asked as he climbed back inside and firmly pulled the door closed.

Larry didn't answer. This didn't look like a town that had been abandoned a few months or even years ago, it looked like it had been decades since it last saw humans.

Cuba wasn't very big and they continued on their way. "St James, next," Brian Gnad said in a tone of false cheer.

"I didn't see the world's biggest rocking chair," Sean joked. No one laughed.

Brian's rail truck moved along, the rain continuing, as if that was all it would ever do in this place. Shaw had to fight a feeling of dread, as if the rain hid something, something that watched them as they drove.

***

Jack dreamed.

It wasn't quite a nightmare. He saw darkness, a cave, he thought, though he wasn't really sure.

He preferred the dream, because when he wasn't deep enough asleep to dream, his chest hurt and his breathing was a labor.

There was something in the cave with him. Something big, something that didn't like him. This wasn't a normal cave, either. It was big, huge, even, big enough that he couldn't sense the walls.

It was cold, too, a bone-deep chill that seemed to suck the warmth from his limbs.

*You aren't supposed to be here,* a soft voice spoke.

Jack felt warmth on his back and he turned. A woman stood there, her features clouded in soft white light. The warmth came from her, heat and light that shook the chill out of him just from looking upon her.

"Who are you?" Jack asked.

She came forward, not seeming to walk, almost seeming to hover. *You don't belong here, Captain.*

"What is this place?" Jack asked. "Who are you; what is..." He could sense the thing in the darkness, it was closer, now. "What is that?"

*It is something old, older than your kind, older than the mountains... and it hates you.* She answered him. He realized that he heard her voice in his mind, he *felt* her words. *You need to come away from this place.*

Jack turned, looking back at the darkness. He could feel the thing here, and now that she had told him, he felt its hate, too. Something moved in that darkness, though it kept entirely out of the light cast by the woman. "Why am I here?"

*Because you sense the threat, and it is in your nature to seek it out, even not knowing,* she answered him. *Come away, my Captain, before it is too late.*

Jack turned back towards her and followed the glowing woman. "Who are you?"

*You know who I am,* she answered, *or at least, you know enough.* They came to a spot of the cave where light shone down from above, high above. Jack found himself drawn up that column of light, rising with the woman.

They went past a platform, partially illuminated as they rose, and Jack made out a sign, *Devil's Well.* They continued to rise, and as they emerged into the light, his companion began to fade away.

"What happens if I need you?" Jack had to ask.

*You don't need me, my Captain, I need you.* He felt the words and then his dream faded and he fell into a deep, restful sleep.

***

Katie bit her lip as Jack's mumbling and thrashing eased. She had become certain that he had internal bleeding, that he might have an infection. He'd developed a fever and she'd hit him with the medicine that she had, though she hated to use any of the precious quantities they had.

Sure, they had recovered Nidal Malak's stash, but it was all pretty much irreplaceable. In the humidity and heat of Missouri, they weren't likely to find much in the way of medicines that hadn't succumbed, or any way to make more.

The first thing she did was check his breathing, her hands as gentle as she could on his chest. His lungs still sounded clear, which relieved her more than she could admit.

He said something, then, her cool hands on his chest. He opened his eyes, his gaze on her face, "My lady," his eyes bore into hers, a moment so intense that it took her breath away.

Then his eyes closed and his breathing eased and he seemed to drop deeper into sleep.

Katie felt a wave of relief. She didn't know *what* had just happened, but she could feel it. A shift. He was going to pull through. She didn't know *how* she knew it; she just did.

Katie bent her head down and rested her cheek against Jack's. His breath came slow and even.

He had saved her, she was not about to fail to do the same thing for him, not for her Captain.

# Chapter Six

"WE NEED HELP," JOSH Wachope heard as one of their scout trucks rolled up. They hadn't been gone even a full hour and he had heard their report.

Sergeant Pape all but fell out of the passenger-side seat, a couple of people having to come forward and support the big former paratrooper.

More of their people had to help Martins from the back. The man had welts all across his skin and bubbles and blisters had begun to erupt on his exposed skin as well.

"Vine monster," Pape shook his head. The big man looked confused and a little out of it.

"Doc!" Josh called, "Someone get Doc Katie!"

They got everyone out of the truck and laid out on the side of the tracks next to the train. Katie hurried out and she seemed to be everywhere at once. "Lift his feet, he's going into shock. You, put that under his head. Get the jar of ointment, the big one, from the hospital car. You, get some clean water, we need to clean their skin. No not just his, *all* of their skin."

She basically gave the men a sponge bath, having them pull their clothing aside and wiping them down with quick motions. The cloth that she used came away with an oily green substance and she had a pile of dirty rags at the end of it. "Burn those," she told someone. "Don't handle it without gloves and burn the gloves, too. And stay upwind when you burn it."

"What's going on?" Josh demanded. He felt like he had lost control of the situation. Four of the five scouts were laid out, now, all of them showing blisters and welts on their skin.

"This stuff, whatever attacked them, it has an oily coating like poison ivy. It was a little bad with Sergeant Pape, but poor Martins was covered in the stuff and I think he's had something like an allergic reaction over and above the skin blistering."

"I think this stuff is heavily alkaline, the plant seems to absorb heavy metals, that might be why it has such an immediate and toxic reaction to their skin," Katie told him. "When it comes down to it, though, I am just guessing."

"Why would a plant have heavy metals?" Josh frowned.

"Well," Luis Cedano had been watching, "lots of plants absorb different things from their environment. And the Ozarks have some really high concentrations of metals; there's lead mines, other mines here. Maybe it is something in the water?"

"Or something in the ground," Katie frowned. "I wish I knew more, but all four of them are having reactions, just like Tony did. We'll probably need to burn their clothing, too, I don't know if this stuff will wash out."

"Good luck finding more clothing in Sergeant Pape's size," Tim Kennedy laughed.

"That's your job," Josh pointed at the logistician.

Tim scowled at him, "I'm not a magician. Let's at least try to wash his stuff before he's left walking around in a towel, okay?"

"Doc?" Josh asked.

"Sure, we can try," she frowned, "in the meantime, I need to get them coated with aloe and hope we got the stuff off them and their symptoms will ease. Poison ivy can last weeks and if their blisters pop, they could get infected." She didn't need to tell him that it would be a bad thing. They only had so much medicine, after all, and what they had was *all* that they had.

All in all, Josh would rather be dealing with possessed than this shit.

48

He tasked some people to help Doc Katie get her new patients back up into the hospital car and then went to talk with Julie Frost. "What the hell happened out there?"

"Sergeant Pape pretty much explained it," The woman shrugged. "Vine monster. It was the size of a car, with vine tendrils the size of telephone poles and lots of little predator vines." The woman shuddered. "It had a nest, or ambush point or something, in a pile of cars over the road. And bones, a big pile of human and animal bones. It was eating people."

Plants didn't eat people. It was an absurd thought. Josh let out a tense breath, forcing himself to consider it. "Okay, I will put out a warning."

"If it matters, I got some really good pictures of it," Julie told him.

"You took pictures?" Josh asked.

"Well, I couldn't shoot it, not at first," Julie answered. "They were in the way. My little Nikon P1000 takes great pictures, no need to futz around with different lenses or anything, quick snaps and then when they were clear of it, I put some rounds from my lever action in the thing. No idea if we hit anything vulnerable, but it didn't seem to like it." She shrugged, "I can transfer the files over, like I've done before, do you want to see them?"

She was so calm about it, so laid back, that it actually helped to settle him out. He had forgotten how she was, calm and collected in the midst of the worst danger. *We have some good people,* he thought to himself.

"Show those pictures to Doc Cedano, maybe he can figure something out," Josh shook his head. "And good job, maybe seeing pictures of this thing will reassure people."

"I doubt it, I wish I'd never see anything like it again for the rest of my life," Julie called over her shoulder as she walked away.

Josh looked around at the trees and plants around them and he couldn't help a crawling sensation of fear as he realized just how narrow their little band of cleared ground was between the train and the walls of green around them.

He went over to a pair of his guard detail, "Put out the word, keep everyone back from the trees."

Josh went up to the Engine Number 2, one of the new ones they had taken from St. Louis. After he climbed in, he checked with their radio operator.

The man wasn't one of their military survivors, he was a ham radio operator who knew how to work the CB radios all their recon trucks had. "Yeah, both trucks are past Cuba, it sounds like."

Josh gritted his teeth at the easy, almost careless reply. "Did they run into any trouble?"

"Nah, no spooky plants for them," The man gave a little laugh, as if he thought he were funny.

Josh scowled at him. "Those spooky plants injured eight people at this point, one of them the Captain. Unless you'd like to be out there scouting for them, keep your head in the game. If anything happens, let me know right away, got it?"

The radio operator flinched back, "I got it, I got it."

Josh realized he probably could have handled that better, but seeing Tyler Pape and his team incapacitated by *plants* left him more than a little off-kilter.

His gut instinct told him that they needed to get ready to move. There was too much wrong about this whole situation. The towns down here were dead. *Plants* were killing people. He never would have thought it, but he actually missed the straight-forward threat of the possessed.

"Put out word to our scouts, there are some sort of predatory vine monsters, about the size of a car, that will try to pull people and animals in to eat them."

The radio operator stared at him for a long moment as if he'd gone crazy.

"Just do it," Josh told the man.

Then, even as he second-guessed himself in doing it, he went to see about sending a scout back the way they'd come... just in case.

\*\*\*

"You see anything?" Sergeant Ronald Shaw called. They had made link-up with the scout truck on the interstate about ten miles from St James, the next town on their way.

"We ain't seen nothing," Fuller called back.

"You haven't seen anything or you have?" Shaw asked impatiently.

"What?" Fuller asked.

Shaw restrained a sigh. Fuller wasn't a former soldier or cop or anything like that. He and his 'crew' had been hoodlums. Shaw wasn't even sure why the Captain kept them around, though they seemed to do their job well enough. They were dangerous, though, dangerous in a way that made Shaw uneasy.

He restrained any urge to correct Fuller's grammar further. "You get the message about this vine monster?"

"Demon trees, vine monsters, this some bullshit, man," Fuller called. "I'd rather be back in the city smokin' undead."

Shaw didn't know about that. Then again, for all that he grew up in St. Louis, or perhaps because of it, he wasn't a big fan of big cities. That hate for them had grown all the more for the fact that they were choked with undead and crazy things.

Now, though, he was really starting to hate these woods.

"We'll continue on, try to keep us in view," Shaw called.

Interstate 44 looked pretty clean, actually, with a few clusters of cars along the side of the road, but none of the accident choked piles of wrecks common to the interstates near cities or in more heavily-populated areas.

Shaw got back in Brian's rail truck and they pulled out. "They didn't see anything."

"Fuller's crew *never* see anything, not unless there's something they want in it," Sean McCune grumbled from the back seat.

Shaw kept quiet, after all he wasn't sure he could wholly disagree.

Ten miles, back in the old times, would take ten minutes or so. They took a full hour, easing along the tracks, keeping an eye out for threats. Despite what he had told Fuller, the other scout's truck got ahead of them, dropping out of sight as the railroad tracks led away from the interstate and then, as they came back, there was no sign of the truck.

"Fuller," Shaw got on the radio.

"Sup?" Fuller answered a moment later.

"I thought I told you to keep us in sight?" Shaw bit the words out.

"Yeah, I know, I know, but we thought we saw something, we're checking it out," Fuller answered.

"Told you," McCune snorted from the back seat.

Brian shot him a look. Shaw didn't want to do this anymore. He didn't feel like he should be in charge. He didn't know why Wachope had selected him for it. *Worry about Fuller some other time,* he told himself.

"Keep going," Shaw grated.

They rolled on. They were coming up on St James, a much bigger town than Cuba. There were overgrown billboards for a winery and a town museum. Shaw looked at the map, which showed the train tracks going through town.

He didn't know if he had it in him to go through another dead, overgrown town like Cuba.

They drew closer. There was a different feel, right away. A cold, ugly, *hostile* feeling.

"Stay alert," Shaw told the others, his gaze going to the upper stories of the downtown area. This town wasn't as overgrown as the last and there was far more in the way of buildings.

The downtown area looked almost untouched. There were a few signs of hasty protection on some buildings, with windows and doors boarded up, though he didn't see any signs of active survivors. "Stop the truck." Shaw ordered as they came into the center of the town.

There was a cold, angry waiting feel to the place, one that put him on edge. "What's that?"

"That" was a big, brick-walled school-building with a tall gymnasium that loomed over the other buildings on the south side of the railroad tracks. There were makeshift walkways thrown up between the school and other nearby buildings. Even as he watched, there was movement around the building and then a set of garage doors rolled up.

"Survivors," Brian said cheerfully.

"Raiders, go, go, go," Sean and Larry called together.

Shaw didn't know how they knew so quickly, but he trusted their instincts. "Gun it, get us out of here."

Brian started the truck moving, even as a squad of dirt bikes roared out of the garage, followed by a big, lifted pickup truck.

"Well, *that's* not good," Lieutenant Baxter said in a dry tone.

"You think?" Shaw asked, even as he watched the dirt bikes quickly reach the railroad tracks and turn sharply and accelerate in their direction. "Can we go faster?"

"Not really," Brian told him, "It's a rail truck, not a race-car."

"Get on the radio to Fuller and to the train, let them know what's going on," Shaw ordered, even as he started to put down the window. He was a lefty, which was going to come in handy just now because he wasn't going to be able to shoot right-handed back at them.

The raiders were coming up fast, a dirt bike with a rider and passenger coming right up alongside, the passenger pulling out a gun of some kind.

Shaw had far more stable of a platform and he shot first. The sharp crack of the rifle in the vehicle cab set his ears to ringing.

He wasn't sure if he hit them or if just the gunfire startled the driver, but the bike swerved hard, turned sideways, and then flipped, sending both riders flying.

Even as that happened, though, two riders came up on the other side and gunfire roared at them.

"They're shooting holes in my truck!" Brian shouted.

"Got it," Larry shouted back as he fired out and across Lieutenant Baxter. His shotgun blast definitely caught both riders, because they went down and their bike rolled in response. It was so loud that the ringing in Shaw's ears became church bells.

"Seriously?" Lieutenant Baxter shouted, "I'm trying to radio the train!"

The lifted pickup was bouncing along the tracks behind them, and in the side mirror Shaw could see a half-dozen men in the bed of it, firing guns at them, though with how the absurd vehicle bounced, he didn't see how they could hit anything.

The track reached the far end of town and started a curve. Two of the dirt bikes raced ahead of them, going flat-out on a side road in a bid to get ahead of them.

The rail truck's engine roared, Shaw readied himself, not sure what the two bikers had planned until he saw them pulling up to a railroad crossing. They could try to block the tracks and fire at them as they tried to get off or avoid them, he realized.

They didn't have time to get off the track. Shaw leaned out the window and fired at the bikers, trying to get them out of the crossing. He wasn't sure if he hit anything or not.

Bullets cracked back at them, but neither of the bikers had time to push anything in the way of the tracks.

Brian's truck rolled over the rail crossing and out of the town, Brian coaxing speed out of the truck as they went. The raiders gave up the chase at the rail crossing, though Shaw wasn't sure why.

"Is everyone okay?" Shaw called, barely able to hear anything over the ringing in his ears.

"My poor truck," Brian patted the dash of his truck.

"We're fine back here," Larry offered.

He looked back at Lieutenant Baxter, who had her headset off and was rubbing at her ears and glaring at Larry, who was still trying to get his shotgun back out of the way.

"Lieutenant, please get on the radio and let the train know there's a group of raiders there in town," Shaw told her. In a way, it was somewhat reassuring that there *were* some survivors there.

Granted, they were a threat they would have to deal with, but that was something they could tackle, something understandable, unlike animated plants.

"Fuller," Shaw used the truck radio, "Fuller this is Shaw."

"Sup, bro," Fuller answered.

"We've got raiders in the town, don't go in, they may have traps and such."

"Yeah, bro, we ran into something, figured that was what was going on," Fuller answered.

Shaw grated his teeth, "You could have warned us."

"It got a little exciting here for a minute. We saw you all getting clear so we kept quiet." Fuller answered. "We'll head back. You going to continue?"

Shaw wanted to go back and beat Fuller's ass, but there was a group of raiders directly between them, so he would have to settle up with the former gangbanger later.

"We'll continue scouting," Shaw bit out.

"Talk to you later, bro," Fuller told them.

Shaw let out a tense breath. They had no support, now. If they couldn't continue on to confirm the rail line was clear, no one else could, at least not until that cluster of raiders got cleared out.

"Is it too late to ask if we can go back to the train?" McCune asked.

"Yes," Shaw looked back at him. "Yes, it is. We're continuing on, unless anyone has any issues with that?"

"We could lift the rail wheels and take the roads, probably even find a way back avoiding the raiders," Brian offered.

"Then someone else, or likely just us again, has to come out and scout again, anyway," Shaw shook his head. "Let's drive on."

He hoped he wasn't making a terrible decision.

***

Fuller wasn't an educated man. He was, however, pretty smart.

He'd never been a big fan of how things ran with the train. Sure, he could admit, the Captain had got them through all kinds of crazy things, from the nightmare back in Cincinnati, to the stuff in St. Louis.

But the Captain didn't dream big. Fuller could admit he kind of liked the setup that Nidal guy had going on. He lived like a king. Fuller might have even thought about signing on with him, only everything he had seen and heard told them that Nidal wasn't going to be the type to share power.

Neither was Fuller, really.

These raiders, though, they gave Fuller an opportunity. The Captain wasn't doing so well. Fuller had seen people hurt like him curl up and die, before and after the dead rose.

With the Captain out, Fuller might have an opportunity to step up. Sure, there were a few people who weren't going to go along with that.

That's what the raiders could be for... and it looked like they had a nice little setup here in town, too.

"Hey there," Fuller grinned at them. Him and his truck were up on the interstate overpass. The raiders had a few guards up here, but his guys had snuck up on them and they wouldn't be causing problems until they woke up. Sherrick had probably hit a couple of them too hard, but Fuller wasn't going to worry if the men never woke up.

Raiders tended to be practical about that sort of thing, after all, it meant splitting the loot a few less ways.

"What do you want?" The guy doing the talking didn't look all that healthy. He looked skinny, with a sort of ill-fed, unhealthy look that Fuller normally associated with drugs.

From the lack of teeth, Fuller was going to guess meth.

"Well, I couldn't help but see that that truck went right through your town, you didn't do nothin," Fuller grinned.

The men down there growled and grumbled at his words, though with how his crew had weapons out and they had the high ground on the interstate overpass, they weren't starting anything. That was how you talked to people, from a position of strength.

Fuller wasn't a great shot, but figured he didn't have to be to hit a few of them from up here.

"You with them?" The raider leader asked.

Fuller shrugged, "Sort of. They got a nice setup and good supplies. What you got?"

"We got women!" One of the other men down below shouted.

Fuller grinned at that. He did prefer women willing, but that was a nice piece of Nidal's setup back in St. Louis, he had women, food, everything he wanted.

"How'd you take the town?" Fuller asked.

"Bunch of religious idiots, offering food, taking people in," the raider leader answered. "Slipped some of my people in and killed anyone who looked able to put up a fight."

Fuller nodded in appreciation. It was something he had thought about doing when he first signed on with the Captain, but the man had never really let his guard down and frankly, he scared Fuller a bit.

Now, though, he was dying and while Wachope scared Fuller a bit, too, he wasn't Captain Jack.

"I could tell you where there's a lot of supplies, people too," Fuller offered. "Maybe I want a place here, a place on your crew."

The man down below smiled, his missing teeth giving him a ghoulish look. "Yeah, that might be a good deal."

The man below was thinking about how to kill Fuller. They both knew it. Fuller was good with that, he was considering the same thing, how to remove him and take over his group.

"So they got military-grade hardware, my man," Fuller began, "and a train, a train with more supplies and loot than you would ever believe..."

# Chapter Seven

THINGS WERE NOT GOING well.

Josh listened to the reports from Sergeant Shaw and a much shorter one from Fuller's team.

Shaw's had the kind of detail that he expected from the young NCO. Josh had been impressed by the younger man, cook or not, he was a good Soldier and a smart, capable man.

Fuller, on the other hand, thought he was smart, but really, he was just clever.

There wasn't much to Fuller's report, not besides that he and his people had seen the raiders and pulled back when he realized they couldn't get through.

Josh Wachope had never really trusted the former gang member. With how tight they were on people, and how Fuller kept in line for Jack, Josh had tolerated him.

He had the feeling that maybe Fuller wasn't going to stay in line.

Unfortunately, their train wasn't in a good spot to defend. They were along a curve, just southwest of Leasburg, and with the dense trees and vegetation, and the lack of open terrain, if Fuller had signed on with these raiders, then they'd know exactly where they were and they'd be able to sneak up through the trees.

He turned to Brockman and Kennedy, "We need to move the train."

"Where?" Brockman protested. "You heard what they said about Cuba, it's... not a good place."

"They didn't see any more of these demon trees or vine monsters there," Josh pointed out. "Anyway, we don't have time to argue about this, Fuller is almost certainly trying to work out some sort of deal with these raiders."

"We don't know for sure..." Tim Kennedy protested.

Josh gave him a level look and the other man shrugged. "Look, I'm not a fan of Fuller, *believe* me, but he can't be stupid enough to think he can work something out with a group of raiders."

Captain Wachope didn't dignify that with a response.

"If we push up here," He went up to the map, pointing at a spot just south-west of Cuba, "There is more open terrain and we and set up to defend better."

"What if there's more of the plant things, there?" Robert Brockman asked.

"Then we deal with them, too," Captain Wachope snapped.

"Why don't we back up, instead?" Kennedy suggested, "There's a couple open spots further back along the rail line..."

"We're not going back," Wachope snapped. He hadn't realized he raised his voice until he saw the other two recoil. He adopted a more moderate tone, "Look, as soon as we start to move back, people are going to get it in their heads that we *can't* continue forwards."

"Maybe we can't," Brockman pointed out. "I mean, there's these... demon plants, the raiders..."

"If anything, the raiders are proof that we *can* survive down that way," Wachope assured him. "If they can survive, so can we. I think the main threat is *here*, and the longer we stay here the worse it is going to get."

"That... well, that makes a certain level of sense," Brockman nodded.

"Look, I hate to say it," Tim Kennedy raised his hands, "I think you need to put it to a vote."

"What?" Wachope asked in shock. He would not have expected either of Jack's two friends to suggest anything like that, not really.

"We've got a lot of new people, a lot of scared people," Tim Kennedy met his gaze. "I'm with you, Robert is with you, but, Josh..." He shook his head.

"If these people start to think you're going to set yourself up as king or something…"

"I'm *not*," Wachope snarled. "God, the *last* thing I want is to be in charge."

"Then tell them that, *show* them that, put this all to a vote, warn them about the raiders, lay it all out and let them vote on a course of action," Tim Kennedy told him in a reasonable tone.

"What happens if they vote to go back?" Wachope demanded.

"Then, what's the worse that happens, we go back, we lose a bit of time, we find out if we can go the other way and…"

"And if we can't, we have to come back this way, only those raiders will know we have to use the tracks. Maybe they tear up the tracks so we can never get through, so we're stuck here," Captain Wachope said in a hard tone. "Or the idiots who want to go south drive us *deeper* into the woods and we really run into something nasty."

The other two were quiet. "Do you distrust us all that much?" Brockman asked.

"I don't distrust *you* two," Josh blinked at him in surprise. As the two stared at him dubiously, he went on, "I don't! I just… you two aren't the only ones voting."

"I think we have a pretty good feeling for how they're going to vote," Tim Kennedy answered. "Especially since we *are* going to try and shape this all. But if everyone's together on this, it's going to go a lot better than if you just order people around."

"Jack orders people around all the time," Josh hated the words as they came out of his mouth.

"He doesn't, not really. He tells, he directs, but he asks, he talks, he cajoles…" Brockman shrugged and looked at Kennedy, who nodded. "He talks to people. You're just running around telling people what do to."

"That's not what I'm doing at all," Wachope protested. He knew better than all of that, besides. He'd served in Special Forces, he knew how to build relationships, how to motivate irregulars, how to...

*How to not do exactly what I've been doing.* The thought hammered him. "Shit."

He'd been feeling out of his depth, he had forgotten everything he knew, everything he had been trained.

"Okay," He leaned back against the windows of the engine cab. "How do we do this?"

"Put out to everyone we are going to put it to a vote in the morning. Lay it out for everyone, the raiders, the evil plants, even this stuff with Fuller," Kennedy said.

Josh Wachope found himself nodding in reply. It made sense. It was hard, though, especially when he knew just how precarious their situation was. His wife, his two young children, their lives depended upon everyone voting together, upon them making the right choice.

He didn't like that. He didn't like it at all. Even when he knew that getting everyone on board was the right thing, he hated it. Because this wasn't some group of locals in a distant country, this was his *family*'s life on the line.

He closed his eyes and let out a deep breath and when he opened them, he gave both men a slow nod. "Alright. I'll go tell everyone. You two do whatever magic you think you need to do."

"We'll talk to people, lay it all out," Brockman nodded. "They'll make the right choice."

Josh Wachope wasn't so sure. They seemed so certain... but what if they were wrong?

***

"Morning Chief, what you up to?" Josh asked, several hours later as he came into the car that housed the train's machine shop. Most of it had been assembled by Paul Montandon, the former mechanic and gunsmith who had helped them get the train going.

He'd heard tools going here, while most of the rest of their survivors were sleeping, and the noise had drawn him.

He had told everyone, moving from car to car, about the upcoming vote. Most of them had taken the news with excitement, though there'd been worry, concern, and even anger at the news that he'd put their course to a vote.

Warrant Officer Tom Knighton was at work with a hammer and what looked like a section of steel plate, moving from the coal forge to anvil, then pounding and shaping before moving it back. They had a gas forge, too, but the gas was hard to find at this point, whereas they found coal just about everywhere.

"Working on something," Chief Knighton answered. There was a smooth, rhythmic motion to his hammer strikes as he moved the steel, heating it, putting hammer to it, and moving it back.

"Working on what?" Josh asked, coming closer. Knighton had said he needed to do something when Josh had asked him to go scouting with the others the previous day. He had accepted that, figuring the man needed some time. He wasn't going to push any of their people past the point of breaking, and Knighton had seen and been through some of the worst of the fallen world.

Knighton didn't answer for a moment, he just continued to hammer the steel, forging it into a curved section of plate before it cooled from white-orange to a darker red, before he put it back into the coal forge.

He cranked the hand-powered fan to warm the coals, his eyes not leaving the steel. "I had a dream, after the Captain got hurt."

"Yeah?" Josh asked. "What, like a nightmare?"

Knighton pulled the metal plate out with his tongs and went back to beating on it, his blows calculated and timed, a perfect metronome as he shaped the metal to form. "When I was younger," he timed his words as he hammered, "I really got into the SCA."

"The what, now?" Josh asked. He didn't know what SCA stood for in military terms.

"SCA, Society of Creative Anachronisms, the guys who dress up in armor, and robes and act out medieval stuff," Knighton answered. He paused his hammering, evaluated the curved plate, and then put it back in the coals and cranked the hand-fan, eying the glow of the coals.

"That led to HEMA, and live steel and some other stuff," Knighton told him. "That was back when I was young and dumb and jumped out of planes for a living. Anyway, I liked beating on other people with pieces of metal, it helped me work out my angry. Then I ran into an old guy, and he trounced me. I mean walked all over me, put me in the hospital for three days, actually, because I didn't know when to stay the fuck down."

"Where are you going with this?" Josh asked, genuinely confused at this point.

Knighton pulled the white-hot steel out of the forge and worked it, a perfect rhythm as he did so, pausing now and then to check it and then, still hot, he put it into the forge, adjusting it around in the core of the heat until he was happy with it, before jerking it out and driving it straight into a bucket of oil.

He looked over at Wachope as he held it in the oil, "After I got out, I went and found the old guy and asked him to teach me. He spent all day hammering metal, he was an armorsmith, a genuine *master* armorsmith, and he had me work the forge every spare moment. I'd get out of the field, wouldn't bother to get cleaned up because I'd go straight to his forge and hammer on steel for the whole weekend and then be back to the barracks. The whole time, he'd talk to me, tell me things about steel, about making armor, about shaping metal and using blades. Guy was a national treasure; he forgot more about moving metal and fighting than I'll ever know."

"I trained with him, off and on, for seven years, two different assignments, there in North Carolina and both times with deployments breaking up the time I had, but every free moment I had spent learning from him," Knighton told him. "He was there training me, working me as much as he would steel, though I didn't realize it at the time. And at the end of it, he got sick, old age caught up, and between one lesson and the next, he was gone."

"So..." Josh frowned as Chief Knighton pulled the curved plate out of the oil and set it down on a stack of other metal plates. They looked like nothing so much as a puzzle. "What are you making?"

"In my dream, he came to me, with a woman in white," Knighton turned to look at him, and Josh was shocked to see tears in the man's eyes. "They said that the Captain wouldn't have been hurt if he had proper armor and that it was time for me to finish the set I'd started making."

***

Captain Josh Wachope sat in the train car he and his family shared with some of the other leaders of the group.

He hadn't really thought about how that might look, particularly to some of the newest survivors. This car, next to the medical car, was one of the better protected ones. They didn't have any luxuries the other cars didn't have. They didn't have more food; they didn't have furniture or creature comforts.

It was just another cargo car, with simple steel walls and wood and steel floor. It was closer to the front of the train and benefited from a few more improvements and protections, a bit of steel plate added as armor back when they had been more worried about raiders and less about the weight of the train.

The interior had a few partitions, sheets hanging from nails and cord to give families some privacy, nothing more than that.

Josh Wachope wasn't thinking about that, though. He found himself thinking about the various conversations he had with people throughout the night.

Most of their military and paramilitary survivors seemed uncomfortable or actively hostile to the idea of a vote. Most of the civilians seemed distrustful of it, as if they didn't trust a vote to be open or for him to honor it.

Even then, he'd heard all kinds of wild suggestions. People wanted to go back to St. Louis. Other people wanted to turn north, to abandon the train, to turn east, to travel on foot. There were suggestions as varied and absurd as he could imagine, most suggested in such serious tones that he knew without a doubt that those suggesting them all believed in their ideas.

Despite the assurances of Tim Kennedy and Robert Brockman, Captain Josh Wachope wasn't all that sure how things would turn out. He sat, the early dawn light coming in through the open door of the train car that he shared with the families of several others, and he stared at the sleeping forms of his two children and his wife.

They didn't have much. A mattress laid down on the steel and wood floor of the car, where they sat while the train rolled, where they slept together at night. A handful of personal possessions they had managed to keep, just enough to fit in their backpacks.

His son and daughter, curled tight against their mother. This was the only world that his youngest would ever know, she'd only been a few weeks old when this all started.

Could he really trust their lives to a vote by people who had only survived through luck or the hard work of others?

The answer, when he thought about it that way, was simple enough.

He got up, moving quietly, though he saw his wife's eyes open and she reached out a hand to him without stirring their children. Josh kissed her hand and slipped away into the early morning light to make preparations... just in case.

# Chapter Eight

"ALRIGHT, LISTEN UP," CAPTAIN Josh Wachope called out to the crowd. The sun was up and he had told everyone they'd do their vote now. He had guards out and replacements so they could come in and vote in turns.

The crowd didn't really quiet, though the murmuring and talking dropped to the point that he could talk over them at least.

"There's four buckets," Josh told them. "I've been passing out stones to each of you; everyone has one stone apiece." They didn't have enough paper to waste to write people's names on each and cast votes that way.

"One rock, one vote," Josh went on. "First bucket is we continue on, take the train tracks to Springfield, then head either southwest to Texas or west." Voices muttered and spoke and he went on over them, "We'll have to deal with the raiders in St James, but we've handled worse."

"Second bucket is we back up to the other tracks back in Pacific," That was almost back in St. Louis. "From there, we try to go straight west to Kansas City."

This time there was more talking and he pitched his voice loud to get over the discussion. "Third bucket," he *really* didn't like this one, but there'd been a persistent group who supported it for some unknown reason, "is we turn *south* at Cuba, we take the tracks as far as they go." They knew exactly how far those tracks went, and they'd be stuck in the middle of the woods.

"Fourth bucket, is everything else. Every other idea, everything from abandoning the train to going back and setting up shop in St. Louis." He couldn't believe anyone would think that was viable, not even after they had destroyed the Hand of God.

"After everyone votes, we'll count the rocks, right here, in front of everyone," Josh told them.

"Come up, one at a time, drop your rock in, like this," He walked forward, dropped his rock in the first bucket and stepped back. "Every adult votes." Some of them had weighed in that adults should vote for their kids or that kids could vote. Many of the kids were below the age of ten, and a lot of them were orphans. Since none of them could agree on the who or the how for either part of that, he had set the cut-off by age. *And if a sixteen year old votes as an adult, I'm not going to complain.*

No one rushed forward to vote. Presented with the opportunity, most of the crowd stood there, uncertainly. *They really don't want to make the decision,* Josh realized, *they want to be heard, they want to be able to complain if someone makes the wrong decision, but they don't want to make the decision themselves.*

His wife came forward and gave him a smile as she dropped her rock in the first bucket. A moment later, Robert Brockman and Tim Kennedy did the same.

Meelah, the woman who'd spoken so much of turning south, stepped forward, her chin high, "South lies safety." She dropped her rock into the third bucket and it thudded into the bottom of the bucket like a lead weight.

People came forward after that. Most of them hesitated, starting to do one thing, looking at the number of the rocks in a bucket, rethinking it. A couple stared at Josh and the other's suspiciously, as if expecting him to tell them to vote one way or another.

He just stood there, waiting; his expression outwardly calm.

Inwardly, he was far from calm. Despite the assurances of others, he saw far more people than he hoped throw their stones in the second, third, and even fourth buckets. This wasn't going to be a clear majority for one course of action. What should have been a simple choice was going to leave a lot of people upset.

It was also taking a lot more time than he wanted to waste. Those raiders weren't all *that* far away and if Fuller had gone over to them, as Josh expected the man had, then they would know exactly where to find the train. They *needed* to move, needed to take action, and instead, the group was taking their sweet time in voting on a course of action.

The morning sun as well up in the sky and it was starting to get uncomfortably hot by the time the last couple of people came forward and dropped their rocks in the buckets.

"Anyone else?" Josh looked around at the group. No one had tried to vote a second time, though he *had* spotted a couple people picking up extra stones from the ground. A dour look at those individuals had quelled the attempt at cheating before they went through with it.

When no one came forward or spoke, he turned to Brockman, "Start counting."

They started on the bucket on the end. Brockman counted out loud, tossing stones over onto the side of the tracks as two men held up the bucket for him. "...one hundred twenty-three, twenty-four, twenty-five... twenty-six. That's it, one hundred and twenty-six, total."

There were mutters and frowns from those who had their own ideas about what to do, but no one shouted or complained.

*Not yet, anyway,* Josh thought darkly.

The next bucket took longer.

The area between his shoulder blades itched as they all stood there, while Brockman counted, tossing stones in to the pile. "Four hundred and fifty, fifty-two, fifty-three, fifty-four." He tipped the bucket over to show it was empty.

Josh barely kept control over his expression. They had fourteen hundred and thirty-four adult survivors, eighteen hundred and eight total when they counted kids. That meant that almost a third of them had voted to turn the train south and head into the woods.

Brockman started up on the second bucket. He had it down to a rhythm now and he went through the process quicker, "...three-eighty-five, three-eighty-six, three-eighty-seven. Three hundred and eight-seven people for going back to Pacific."

Josh did the math in his head even as he tallied who was here, who *couldn't* be here, and who might not have voted. His stomach had gone tense and he hoped he was wrong, even as he felt his blood pressure climb. *Please let me be wrong, please...*

There were four others scouting with Sergeant Shaw, six others with Fuller's truck. Doc Katie hadn't left Jack's side in the hospital car... and Jack wasn't in any sort of shape to come out. Besides them there were three hundred and sixty-four children, none of whom could vote.

Brockman continued counting, though his pace had slowed and he kept pausing, almost as if he didn't want to finish.

He was coming to the bottom of the first bucket, now, "Four hundred fifty, fifty-one, fifty-two... he reached around, found another, "Fifty-three." He tipped the bucket over, empty. "Total is four hundred and fifty-three."

He looked over at Josh, his expression one of dawning horror, "Captain Wachope, I count four hundred and fifty-three votes for continuing on. Four hundred and fifty-*four* for turning south at Cuba."

He didn't have the chance to go on. People started shouting. One man came forward, protesting that he wanted a recount, which was absurd since everyone had been there for the count and the stones had been thrown to the ground.

Josh's mouth tasted like ashes. This, in many ways, was *worse* than what he had expected. He didn't know how they could be so short-sighted, so foolish.

Meelah moved forward, "We have voted, we have chosen. We will turn south, and take the tracks as far as they go!"

There were some cheers, though most people stared at her, uncertain, worried. Maybe a lot of them were rethinking their decision.

It didn't matter to Josh at this point. Just as they had made their decision, he had made his.

As people went to their train cars and many milled in uncertainty, he caught his wife by the hand and pulled her along to their car. Some of his people were already there, gathering their things.

"What's going on?" Heather asked in confusion.

"They made their choice, we aren't going with them," Josh answered.

"We're... what?" Heather asked in shock.

"Get our kids, get our things, we're leaving. I'd already talked to the others and..." Down the way, he saw Johnny Woodard and Sergeant Pape carrying a stretcher out of the hospital car on the far side of the train from the gathered people, out of their sight. Doc Katie looked confused as she followed them. "We don't have long. If the others figure out we're abandoning them, we might have a riot."

"We *can't*..." Heather protested. "These are our friends, our companions, our kids play with theirs and..."

"They wanted a vote, they got it," Josh growled.

His wife stared at him in shock and he let out a tense breath, "Heather, if we stay here, if we go with them, we're going to be going into that forest," he waved an arm at the woods, "We have multiple people injured from it already. I don't know what's in there, I don't know what's going on there, I have no *idea* why anyone, much less several hundred of our people, would want to go there."

He met her gaze and put every ounce of certainty in his voice, "I do know, that if we go with them in there, we're all going to die. I can't save everyone; I *can* save a few of us. And, God willing, if Jack pulls through, he might be able to get them to change their minds and turn around, but right now, if I *do* step in and force the issue, we *will* have a riot and our little group will not survive what I have to do. So please, get our kids, get our stuff and *move*."

***

71

Robert Brockman was... well, he wasn't really sure what to think. He trusted people, most of the time, to think, to use their heads.

Sure, he had seen people do some pretty stupid things before, but he and Tim had been talking to everyone, laying things out, going over their options.

He never, not in a hundred years, would have expected so many people to make such a bad choice.

"Alright, let's get this train moving!" Meelah came into the engine cab, her voice excited. A half-dozen people followed her. The space wasn't really laid out for that many people and they brought with them noise and chaos in a fashion that made him flinch back.

"Uh, why are you here?" Robert asked.

"We went with my plan, that makes me in charge," Meelah told him. "There's going to be a few changes, of course, I'll need some quarters up here near the front of the train, and access to our supplies. Some of my supporters have some requirements as well, greater access to weapons and supplies, for one thing."

"Uh, we voted on a course of action, not a leader," Robert told her. Tim wasn't back yet; he had gone to get his wife settled.

"That's a trivial detail," Meelah snapped. She gestured at one of the men who'd followed her, "Thayvan, make sure he gets the train moving. Where are the lists of supplies?"

The woman went over to the neat, orderly stacks of paperwork and started rifling through them, "I know you all have been keeping the best stuff for yourselves..."

"Uh, we really haven't..." Robert began.

The tall man she'd sent in his direction glowered at him. "Get the train running."

"Uh, just because we voted on..."

The man punched him. The blow caught Robert by surprise and he toppled backwards, landing on his backside and staring up at the man in shock.

"Not too hard, we need him... for now," Meelah called.

"Where's the stashes of booze, medicine?" She rifled through the papers. "Ugh, Shamika, come look through this stuff, see where they keep the good stuff."

"Yes, of course," one of the hangars-on came forward and she started sorting through the papers. If anything, she was worse than Meelah as she started tossing papers left and right as she pawed through them. "Ugh, baby formula? You all track this, seriously? Lame." She crumpled that page up into a ball and threw it out the open door.

"I said," Meelah turned to look at Robert, "get the train moving."

"We don't know if everyone is onboard, there are checks we need to make..." Robert Brockman trailed off as she laughed.

"Oh, do you think I *care*? They voted; we're going south. I got them stirred up to oust the current leadership; I got them worried and afraid. You and your friends, you thought that appealing to logic and reason was going to convince people. I appealed to their fear, their worry. So long as I keep them all off balance, afraid, worried, they're going to keep doing what I say." Meelah laughed, "That's what I learned from the Lord Protector and his Hand of God... and that's what I will do here."

She tapped Thayvan on the shoulder, "Now, get the train started or I'll have him start breaking bones in your left hand until you do what I say. You don't need both hands to operate the train, right?" She smiled venomously.

Robert stood up, slowly. Out of the corner of his eye, he saw trucks pulling away. They were the armored military vehicles, and somehow, without looking, without even thinking about it, he knew those trucks probably carried Captain Wachope and most of the other military survivors.

He really hoped they also had Captain Jack with them

"Marrik, take a few people and go to the hospital car, make sure the *Captain* is comfortable," Meelah's smile suggested that she didn't mean anything of the sort.

This was bad, Robert Brockman realized. It was worse, far worse than he had ever thought it could go, and it had gone that way far faster than he had expected.

Meelah had clearly had a plan; she'd used the vote to set up a sort of take-over. He didn't know what kinds of promises or bargains she had made, but the civilians with her seemed willing to go along with her.

"Get the train going," Meelah snapped. "Or we start breaking fingers. Thayvan, start with his pinky."

Robert wanted to do anything else, however, he also knew that the threats would only escalate. And his wife was here. He went through the engine startup, even as he kept a watch, out of the corner of his eye, as the three military and two other trucks drove out of sight.

He really hoped that wasn't the last he would see of them.

***

Meelah had planned this little takeover for the past few weeks, ever since she'd slipped in with this lot after they took down the Lord Protector.

She didn't really miss her former master. She certainly didn't miss the Hand of God.

Meelah *did* miss the jewelry, the fresh food, the soft bed. She missed how she'd been treated as one of Nadal Malik's concubines, even one of the least of them.

Not enough to go back, of course. She had seen what the Hand of God did to people, she didn't want to have the life sucked out of her, she certainly didn't want to be a possessed.

The train presented her an opportunity. Nadal Malik had showed her the way. Keep people afraid and uncertain. Offer them all sorts of promises, the more absurd and fanciful, the better. The south, safety and security, a land of promise. That had been the honey she had tempted the fearful with. It was a

74

trap, of course. She knew it was a dead-end, the train would hit the end of the tracks, she'd disable it out there, too, just in case... then they'd be stuck.

There were some towns there, though, and they had enough people on the train to work as labor to clear land, establish another plantation, and buy security...

*Oh, right,* she thought

"Radio?" Meelah held out an imperious hand.

"Here you are," One of her crew brought over a CB handset on a long cable.

"Fuller, Fuller, you there?" Meelah asked. She didn't bother with call-signs or anything like that. She and Fuller had worked things out already.

"Yeah, yeah, I'm here," Fuller's tone wasn't the friendly, helpful one she would have preferred. "You made your move?"

"These idiots had a vote, I did what I had to do to get the votes I needed," Meelah laughed. "Those raiders out there any use?" The rumors that he might have gone over to the local raiders had made people all the more fearful, it had worked better than she could have hoped.

"Bunch of meth-addled hillbillies," Fuller answered. "You want me to try and hire them on or just ditch them?"

She considered it for a moment. In truth, she didn't much trust *Fuller*, for all that the pair of them had already talked about taking over.

The raiders he'd found might be a useful bit of muscle to keep people in line, or they might try to take over, or she might use them to kill Fuller and take over his crew...

*Nah,* she thought. "Just ditch them and meet me in Cuba. Be sure you switch the tracks over, too."

"We're going south?" Fuller's voice sounded nervous over the radio.

"Yeah, there's a town up there, where the tracks end. We're going to rule over it."

"You ain't worried 'bout them trees?" Fuller definitely sounded nervous. *He's soft,* she thought, *weak... I should rid myself of him as soon as possible.*

Meelah stared into the woods beyond the engine's windows. She didn't see a threat; she saw an opportunity. She didn't care if the woods killed a few or even a couple hundred of the people on the train. There were too many mouths to feed as it was.

She was going to rule over them, a queen, adored, feared, and worshiped. The tattoo that Nidal had put on her chest seemed to pulse even as she thought of it.

"There's nothing to worry about at all," she smiled as she said those words. "Now get your ass back here."

# Chapter Nine

"I CAN'T BELIEVE YOU just abandoned them all," Katie protested.

She and Josh sat in the back of the Cougar MRAP. Between them, atop a pile of supplies and a stretcher lashed down in place, lay Captain Jack Zamora, still unconscious.

"What else was I supposed to do?" Josh sat across from her. His eyes were sunken, with exhaustion and worry and as he stared at her, she wasn't sure if he even saw her. "Take over after I promised we'd put it to a vote? Shoot anyone who didn't go along with it?"

Katie looked away from the Soldier's dark eyes. There was more to his question than mere sarcasm. There was actual *question* in his words, as if he had considered doing just that.

She wasn't entirely sure she disagreed with it, either. Certainly, there was only so far that a threat of force would go. If people had argued and it turned to violence... how far should he have gone to force them to follow his direction?

"Where are we going?" Katie changed the subject. "We can't survive on our own... five trucks, whatever supplies you have..."

"We could, I planned for this contingency, just in case, we've got two months supplies of food, enough food to push out west, and maps to trains left parked in remote areas, places we can resupply, assuming we can even make it away from the woods."

There was an edge to his voice as he said that, one of uncertainty.

"Look," he didn't meet her gaze as he went on, "I wanted to take everyone I could, believe me. But I was standing there, early this morning, thinking about the worst that could happen, about what someone like Fuller might do if the vote went in their favor..." He shrugged. "First thing someone like that would do would be make sure Jack didn't recover."

"What?" Katie asked in surprise. "What makes you think..."

He gave her a level look, "I did some really crazy things with the Army for five years in the Special Forces. Part of the training goes into how to destabilize and overthrow power structures. I don't for a minute believe that Fuller going rogue and this voting thing coming to a head all at the same time is a total coincidence. Someone got people moving, someone influenced things. We had close to five hundred people join us from Nadal Malik's survivors... who's to say we didn't end up with some bad ones?"

Katie frowned, "I would have told you if there were any of his lieutenants or anything..."

"You knew every one of his people? You could identify every one of his lackeys, even the ones who managed his books or oversaw workers in the field? You tracked all the women who slept with him?" Captain Wachope asked.

She frowned, "I mean... well, no." There were close to six hundred people, maybe more, who followed him, voluntarily or otherwise. Jack's people had rescued anyone willing to come with them. "Most of Malik's fighters went to the ambush point for the northern rail tracks, right?"

"Sure... but someone had to stay back to watch things. The guards, we dealt with them, but that doesn't mean we got all of them, and for any of his support staff, they could have joined in with the ones he kept as slaves and we probably never noticed."

Captain Wachope's words had a ring of truth to them as she considered it. They had done a cursory screen of the people they had rescued, and she'd helped to screen out a couple of his guards who she recognized, but there might have been others, people she never saw locked up in his little hospital.

"Okay, what are we going to do?" Some part of her had come to the point where she viewed all this as military triage. She could only save the people she could save. Right now, that was the ones here with her.

"Take side-roads west, bypass the raiders in St James, try to find Sergeant Shaw's recon truck," Captain Wachope told her. "Get the Captain somewhere he can heal up, keep him safe..."

He looked up at her. "He gets better, we go back to the train, we pull them out of whatever mess they find themselves in."

"If he doesn't?" Katie asked in a small voice.

Josh Wachope looked down at the still form of the Captain. "Then we get as far away from this accursed place as we can and we pray for the souls of those that didn't."

***

"I'm glad you're seeing reason," Fuller sat down at the table with the raider boss, Eddie.

He and his crew had come inside their place, and he actually liked most of what he saw. Sure, they had some stupid crap like people stapled to the walls of their little fort, but Fuller guessed they did that to keep the others in line.

*They'll die and rise as possessed and then he'll have to deal with them,* Fuller thought.

Still, the raiders had taken the place over from the previous owners, which meant they had some nice gardens growing food and they had clean water from a pump. The raiders had far more armed people than Fuller would have expected, too, close to thirty men and women, with an impressive number of firearms among them.

Fuller's eyebrows went up as a woman sat at the table next to the raider boss.

"This is Jazzy," the raider leader told him. "I'm Eddie Needle."

"Sup," Fuller told her. She was a tall woman, with half the side of her head shaved and a nasty scar running down the side of her face. It looked almost like a burn scar.

The raider leader, Eddie Needle, was a thin man, with sunken cheeks and missing teeth. Up close, Fuller could see the man's hands tremble a bit, either from excitement or possibly drug addiction. *I wonder if the idiot is cooking meth in one of these buildings?*

Fuller smiled at them, "You got a nice place out here, could be a lot nicer with more people and some help." He'd never liked meth, though back in the day he'd dealt it on the streets. A nice joint, though, that he missed, getting stoned and not having to think or feel.

"More people are more mouths to feed," Eddie snarled. "Why would we want that?"

"More people could make your fort a little bigger, grow more food, right?" Fuller asked.

Eddie started to lean forward to argue, but Jazzy put a hand on his arm. *Interesting,* Fuller thought to himself, *looks like his girlfriend really runs the show.*

"What are you suggesting?" Jazzy asked. She had husky voice, a sexy voice. *Shame about her shaved head and that scar,* Fuller thought.

"We've got a train, fifteen hundred survivors, lots of supplies," Fuller told her. "Their leader had a run-in with some sort of killer plant; he's badly injured, probably dying..."

He didn't miss how Eddie looked over at Jazzy when he said that. They knew something, or enough, anyway, that the mention of a killer plant didn't spook them.

"Friend of mine is taking over, but I could always strike a different deal, if you know what I'm saying," Fuller grinned at them.

"You want our help to take the train?" Needle grinned back, his missing teeth giving him a predatory look. "What about your friend?"

"I can always make new friends," Fuller told him.

"What's in it for us, assuming we help you take over?" Jazzy asked in her husky voice.

"They got guns, military grade stuff they took from a warlord in St. Louis," Fuller told them. "Lots of supplies, fuel..."

"We cook methanol here, we don't need no gas," Needle sneered.

*Sure, just methanol, not using it for anything else, right?* Fuller thought. He figured these idiots were probably making meth, though who knew what they were making it out of. Maybe they were drinking the methanol, too. He wouldn't put it past them.

"Still, guns and supplies, that would help you take more stuff, right?" Fuller asked.

The pair of them nodded, though Fuller didn't like how sharp Jazzy's eyes looked. Her boyfriend might be drugged out, but she didn't seem blunted by the drugs.

"So let's talk it out, you all get ready to come help me out when I need it, I set aside a fair share of guns and supplies for you all, people too, if you want them," Fuller told the pair of them. He wanted the train, wanted to continue west, find a good-sized city and set himself up as king.

*King Fuller, has a nice ring to it,* he thought.

"I've got to get back to the train, but we'll be in touch," Fuller told them as he stood up. "When the time comes, I'll let you all know what the plan is."

"Sure, sure," Eddie gave a little giggle and Jazzy gave him a nod.

Fuller backed out, conscious of where the pair's armed guards were and where his own people were as they went back outside to their truck. There had always been the chance that they'd chose to try and kill him, despite any precautions and assurances.

There was a good chance they'd try the same thing if he did call on them.

Fuller would come up with a plan for that, too, though.

Captain Josh Wachope dismounted from his truck, feeling tired, depressed, and overwhelmed.

They'd taken back roads around St James, not that there *were* many roads in this part of Missouri. In some areas vines and trees had begun overgrowing everything, which combined with the news of murderous plants, had made the drive extra nerve-wracking.

To make it all worse, he kept wondering if he should have stayed, if he should have forced the issue or refused the vote.

*Too late to rethink it now,* he told himself.

All of the military and most of the police and emergency personnel survivors and their families were with them. The three military trucks and two diesel-powered civilian vehicles had pulled up at an intersection, what had been a church, next to a set of industrial buildings overgrown with vines.

Most of the land out here looked like farmland, some of it even looked planted closer to the town.

As he dismounted, Sergeant Shaw got out of his truck and to Captain Wachope's surprise, a woman climbed out of the back cab, a woman he hadn't seen before.

She was tall and thin, with blonde hair pulled back in braids.

"Sir, this is Doctor, uh, Arden," Shaw introduced her.

"Doctor?" Captain Wachope asked with narrowed eyes.

"Doctor of Agriculture and Forestry," She answered with a friendly smile. "I've sort of become a leader for our town at this point."

"Town?" Captain Wachope realized he probably sounded like an idiot, asking single word questions. He was so caught off-balance by all this, though, that he had difficulty doing more than that.

"We got past St James and as we came up to Rolla, we found out the town has survived. They've dealt with the possessed problems they had, they're growing crops, sustaining themselves, and they've fended off a few raiders as well, at this point, sir," Sergeant Shaw told him.

"So you just brought their leader to meet us?" Captain Wachope couldn't help but ask in a disapproving tone.

"I *asked* him to bring me to meet you, yes," she told him. "He had told me that there's some sort of... internal issue with your people, I want to make sure it doesn't spill over into my community."

"There's other survivors down here, sir," Sergeant Shaw told him quickly. "They're a bit... concerned, too, because I guess they've held out at Fort Leonard Wood. It's a group of military survivors. Things between them and Rolla are a bit tense right now."

"They demand food, supplies, and they want to recruit our people to form an army," Doctor Arden stated in a harsh tone. "Their leader, Colonel Sinclair, seems to think that we are all under military control."

"That... complicates things," Wachope shook his head. "Look, I don't know what's going on here, I sure don't want to get involved in any local disputes. Right now, we're just trying to figure out our next move."

She stared at him in a long moment of consideration. He couldn't fight the feeling that she was far more perceptive, far more aware, than most people.

After a long moment, she gave a slight nod of her head. "I will let you and Sergeant Shaw catch up. I'll wait to the side, here, part of why I asked for the ride here was to survey what's left of the fertilizer plant to see if we could get it operational again." She nodded at the overgrown structure and she walked in that direction.

"Do you need any protection?" Captain Wachope asked.

"I will be fine, I'm sure," She called back without slowing her pace.

Wachope shook his head, really hoping that some possessed or killer plant didn't knock off the local leader under their watch. He gestured at Johnny Woodard and Sergeant Tyler Pape to follow her, just in case.

"Alright, what the hell is going on?" Captain Wachope demanded.

83

"We got past the raiders there in St James, then we hadn't gone all that far and we ran into an outpost on the edges of Rolla. It took a bit of convincing to assure them we weren't with the raiders up there; I guess they were in contact with St James right up until the raiders moved in a few weeks ago."

"Okay, what's their setup look like?" Josh Wachope asked.

"They're... well, they've survived surprisingly well, sir, I couldn't believe it, really. They've consolidated down onto the university campus, for the most part, but they've got farms going. They weren't exactly sharing a ton of information with us and we didn't get a chance to go see much, not before I got your call, but there has to be a few thousand survivors here, maybe more."

"A few *thousand*?" Captain Wachope asked in shock.

When the dead had risen, things had fallen apart quickly. Any town with more than ten or twenty thousand people had quickly fallen apart. One undead killed one person, that person rose and two undead killed two more. It took a lot of damage to take down the undead, far more than the old movie-style headshots. Blades and blunt weapons worked better than guns, but that took a willingness to get within arm's reach... and by the time people understood that most cities were being overrun.

Some cities had held out, like Chattanooga down in Tennessee, but most cities and towns that had held out had slowly succumbed to the masses of undead, especially out east where there were tens of millions... and where there were other things, terrible things.

*Stuff like the Hand of God... and like in Cincinnati where blood rained from the sky and horrible things dragged people screaming into the water of the Ohio River.*

"Why aren't they on the radio?" Captain Wachope had to ask. "Same for the military survivors, we haven't heard anything."

"Well, for the folks in Rolla, sir," Shaw shrugged, "They just seem to be want to left alone. I don't think they want to advertise their presence, and everything they're doing is to camouflage that they're even here. We didn't even *see* their outpost, not until we were right up on it, they had planted trees and brush around it, they had us dead to rights and it's only the fact that they *didn't* shoot first that I'm still here to talk about it."

"What about Fort Leonard Wood, this Colonel Sinclair?" Captain Wachope asked. He didn't really know how he felt to hear that the installation had held out. Nidal Malik had pretended to be military, he and his thugs *had* been military... though they'd been escaped from the military prison at Leavenworth.

"I don't know the details, sir. I've been receiving some static on our channels, bouncing here and there..."

Josh nodded, "They've got encrypted radios, then, different encryption than us." The radio sets they had, all their military radios, shared certain frequencies and there would be some overlap, even if they weren't using exactly the same ones.

"You haven't gone to meet them, yet?" Captain Wachope asked.

"I haven't had time, sir, we heard your message this morning after we'd made contact with the folks here in Rolla, and honestly..." Sergeant Shaw hesitated.

"You aren't going to offend me," Captain Wachope told him.

Sergeant Shaw looked at the ground. "There aren't all that many military left, sir. Most of us died fighting. Most of the senior officers went down in the thick of it or... well, they ran."

That wasn't something that Josh liked to think about. Captain Jack and him had seen the senior officers from Third Infantry Division hold out on a bridge, the Division Commander and his staff dying to buy civilians long enough to escape.

Not all of the military leadership had been so brave, though. There'd been cases where officers had abandoned civilians or even their units, to escape.

In some ways, Wachope felt painfully guilty as he thought about how he had left the train. *I didn't have a choice,* he told himself. His staying there would have just meant that either things devolved into a bloodbath or he would have had to go along with the new leadership.

Shaw shrugged, "The locals aren't fond of this Colonel Sinclair. I guess he sends convoys over, trying to get people and food to build his army. I haven't heard his side of things, sir, but... well, it sounds a little too much like Nidal Malik for me to be comfortable with it."

It did. Maybe if Josh had a better position, he would have felt comfortable sending a truck to link up with the military at Fort Leonard Wood. Certainly, at one point in time, he knew that both him and Jack Zamora would have done so, happily turning over their band of survivors to someone senior.

Only now... they'd seen what Nidal Malik had done. The man had done worse than set himself up as a warlord. He had actively embraced the evils that had come to their world. He'd worked with the undead, *controlled* them.

They didn't know anything about the military survivors at the installation. There might be a perfectly legitimate reason why a senior officer was still alive. There also might not be.

"How's the Captain?" Shaw asked.

"Doc Katie is with him," Josh answered. His friend had seemed better, though he had been asleep the entire trip. For that matter, Woodard and Pape had said he hadn't so much as stirred as they moved him out of the hospital car.

Even as he thought that, he looked back to see their Doctor climbing out of the vehicle. She came over, squinting a bit in the bright sunlight. "What's going on?"

"Sergeant Shaw brought one of the local leaders here to meet us," Captain Wachope told her in a dry tone. He could see the NCO wince a bit at that. *He should have at least told me.*

"It seems the town of Rolla has held out, they've got a few thousand survivors, they're farming the area. They're staying off the radio to avoid attention," Captain Wachope shrugged, "there's also military survivors at Fort Leonard Wood, who seem to be at odds with the civilians. I gather half of why she came out here was to see if we were connected to them somehow."

"Are we?" Doc Katie asked.

"Not yet," Josh told her.

"Good, because Jack is awake, and he wants to talk with you," Doc Katie told him.

Captain Wachope felt a surge of relief and worry at the same time. Relief that his friend was awake and deep worry over what he would think about what had happened.

He hurried over to see what his friend had to say.

# Chapter Ten

JACK LAY, PROPPED UP a bit, in the back of the MRAP. After his strange dreams, he had fallen into a deep sleep and he didn't remember *anything* between then and when he had woken up, just after the truck had come to a stop.

Katie had filled him in somewhat, the vote, Josh Wachope's decision to take him and escape, in broad terms. She hadn't known details, because she'd been at his side the entire time.

Jack could fill in those details well enough. Someone, probably this Meelah woman, one of their new rescues from St. Louis, had decided to seize power while he was down and out.

Josh looked exhausted and overstrained. His long-time friend had bags under his eyes and an almost hangdog expression. "You have no idea how happy I am to see you awake."

"You have no idea how relieved I am to *be* awake," Jack answered, his mind going to the strange dreams, the monster in the underground lake, the lady in white.

There had been one last thing, too, half-dream, half-vision... a sword.

Jack shook those thoughts off. "What's going on here? Why have we stopped, and please tell me you're thinking on how to go back and take the train?"

"The situation is complicated, Jack," His friend answered. "I can't go back and take the train, not without basically hijacking it, not right now, anyway. It gets more complicated here, there's several thousand survivors in Rolla, they're organized around the college campus, I guess, and they're pretty well set up, from what Sergeant Shaw told me."

Jack's eyebrows went up in surprise. The most survivors they'd found in any one place had been the ones in St. Louis, and even then, it had only been five hundred. There had been a few enclaves holding out on the East Coast, but most of them had gone radio silent in the past months. The city of Chattanooga was holding out, though they hadn't been too vocal about how many people they had there.

"It gets *more* complicated; there are some military holdouts at Fort Leonard Wood. Colonel Sinclair, he runs the base and he's at odds with the locals, demanding supplies and recruits."

Jack's mind locked up on the name. "Did you... did you say *Sinclair*?"

"I did..." Wachope frowned, "You know him?"

Jack had to fight a ripple of unease, "Yeah. I know him. Well, I *knew* him, when he was Lieutenant Colonel Sinclair, my Battalion Commander two years ago." He didn't bother to hide his tone, "I was company commander under him for a year. I hadn't heard he made Colonel."

"The local woman didn't seem to know much military rank, she could have got that part wrong," Josh Wachope shrugged He clearly considered what Jack had said and what he hadn't and the tone in which he had said what he did.

Katie, equally observant, spoke up, "I am guessing you knowing him isn't a good thing... for all of us?"

Jack lay back on the stretcher, his hands moving to his chest and poking and prodding his ribs as he considered what to say. There wasn't the stabbing pain that he had felt after his injury. In fact, while he felt sore and sensitive, he didn't really *hurt*. It would have surprised him, except he had rather a lot to think about and not dying from shattered ribs was a good enough thing that he wasn't going to spend too much time worrying about it.

"We didn't get along. He was... well, *particular* is one way to put it. You either met his biases and expectations or you didn't," Jack told them.

"He's the one you had issues with, then?" Josh Wachope asked in a quiet tone.

Jack only nodded.

"What does he mean?" Katie asked.

Jack sighed. "There's not a lot to say. I ran my company the way I thought I should. My Battalion Commander, Lieutenant Colonel Sinclair, wanted me to do things his way."

"You didn't?" Katie asked. "I thought the Army was big on following orders?"

"We are... but there's things you can't put down as orders, and there's supposed to be a lot left to the initiative of lower leaders," Jack answered. He made a face, still not really comfortable with bad-talking his nominal superior. "His first day on the job, after his change of command, he had us form up out on the parade ground for a talk about his vision and expectations."

"That's fairly normal," Josh Wachope nodded.

"He talked for six hours," Jack told him. "Everyone standing in the sun while he stood at a shaded podium."

"Six..." Josh shook his head.

"We had twenty people fall out from heat injuries," Jack noted. "That was only from *my* company, I can't tell you how many from the whole battalion. He had a whole slew of training that he wanted after that. Book reports, sensing sessions, all kinds of things, stuff that just ate up time."

Jack closed his eyes, "My soldiers got really tired of it. They were combat engineers, not college kids. So I scheduled us out in the field for ranges and field training. Back-to-back, so we just weren't there in garrison for him to interfere."

"Huh, clever," Josh nodded. "What did he do?"

"Assigned me book reports and additional training that he expected us to do, regardless. And he counseled me, that he wanted every Soldier in my company to pass tests, written tests, on the subject material."

"What?" Wachope looked shocked.

"I didn't think he was serious, but after six weeks in the field, we came out and he had tests printed out for us," Jack shrugged. "When about a third of my company failed his special tests, he gave me a negative counseling."

"I think I know where this is going..." Katie shook her head. "This is why you didn't get promoted?"

"He couldn't relieve me, but he used the negative counseling forms, and he ended up with a stack of them, to tank my eval under him. I went from one of the best rated company commanders in the Brigade to one of the worst." Jack told her. "That was pretty much it for my chances to get promoted. By the end of it, I didn't even *care* about promotion. I was so pissed off at the Army, pissed off at my leadership, that I just wanted out."

"And this is the guy that's in charge of the installation?" Josh Wachope shook his head. "So I'm guessing name-dropping you isn't going to help our situation?"

Despite himself, Jack gave a laugh. His ribs twinged a bit, though again he didn't feel any stabs of real pain. "No, I don't think that would be the best thing to do."

He started to sit up and Katie was there, "You really shouldn't."

"I feel *much* better; here, feel." He guided her hands down to his ribs. She dug those fingers in hard, a clear sign that she wanted to show him that he really *shouldn't* get up. Yet when he didn't so much as wince in pain, she frowned and ran hands across his ribs, "You're... healed?"

"Great bedside care," Jack smiled at her.

She smiled back, though she looked confused more than anything else.

He finished sitting up. "Let's get everyone together, I'll talk to this local leader, and then we have to figure out how to save our people."

"What if they don't want to be saved?" Josh asked in a worried tone.

Jack's mind went to the dark cave, the huge underground lake, and the massive *thing* inside of it. It was a feeling he had, a premonition. That place was real. The thing that hungered was there... waiting.

South.

South was where their train and people had gone. South was where this threat lay.

"They're going to need us, whether they know it yet or not," Jack assured him.

***

As it was, Doctor Arden had already departed back to her town. Sergeant Shaw let them know as they came up, that someone had rode up on horses and that she had gone with them while Jack and the others were talking.

"Strange bunch," Jack looked in the direction of the town. Rolla lay in a valley, a fold in the hills that held a broad stretch of farmland. The town itself was wrapped in trees, many of the homes and houses hidden. The taller buildings of the college campus and downtown barely stood over the trees.

He walked slowly, still feeling a bit wobbly on his feet after being out for a couple of days.

"Is this everyone?" Jack asked as he leaned against the front of one of their Joint Light Tactical Vehicles. He needed the support more than he wanted to admit.

"Chief Knighton is working on something," Josh told him, falling into the role of his second-in-command without hesitation.

Chavez had filled that role, often enough as well, but the fireplug NCO had died helping rescue survivors from the prison back in Jacksonville, Indiana. Just as so many other men and women had died under his command.

He couldn't let the rolls of the dead overwhelm him or he might well shut down. Instead, he looked around at the living, the men and women who entrusted him with their survival... and the resources he had to try and rescue the survivors at the train.

There was Captain Josh Wachope, his friend and second in command. The tall man had more tactical acumen and knew how to lead and fight. He'd brought his wife and small children when he led the escape from the train.

Jack knew that his friend blamed himself for how things had gone while Jack was out. In Jack's mind, though, it wasn't Josh's fault... it was his own. Jack should have been more careful, shouldn't have allowed himself to be injured, and he should have had better preparations back at the train in case something *did* happen to him.

Josh's wife, Heather, stood next to him, and their two young children were with her. He didn't know much about her, but the way she stood next to her husband told him that she supported him.

There was Johnny Woodard, the big, half-black, half Korean, former Combat Medic had been a solid presence since he joined up with them. He hadn't been in the army more than one enlistment and he had never made NCO, and that time had been twenty years earlier. But he had worked as a bouncer, a boxer, and paramedic, so he knew plenty about the use of force and how to keep his head in a stressful situation.

Sergeant Tyler Pape was a former paratrooper who, like several others, had got out. He was as big or bigger than Johnny Woodard. Something had happened to his uniform since Jack had been injured, though, and now he wore a pair of board shorts that looked like ranger panties on him and a floral-pattern shirt. That was probably the only clothing they could find for him. The fact that he still managed to look fearsome in such a getup said plenty about him.

Sergeant Ronald Shaw, Brian Gnad, Sean McCune, and his pal Larry all were well known elements and Jack was happy to have all three of them, even if the two salvagers could be as much hindrance as help at times.

Lieutenant Stephanie Baxter, as quiet and professional as always sat with her radio sets, her expression serene, though Jack knew she was about as introverted as possible and that she absolutely hated dealing with people in groups. Her very presence here, rather than being off working on her radios, showed that she really wanted to help, even if she hated being in a group.

Martin and Stein were two of the only junior enlisted to make it this far. Private Joe Martin had bruises and blisters all over his skin, and he had clearly lost his uniform as well. He was a tough kid, from Montana, and he mostly kept to himself and did as he was told. He was a country boy and he looked comfortable in the pair of jeans and t-shirt that he wore.

Private Marty Stein was his almost constant companion, he was from the Bronx, and he almost never stopped talking. Again, like Sergeant Pape and Martin, he'd lost his uniform somehow and he wore a set of baggy pants a couple sizes too big with a belt holding them up and a t-shirt that hung off his small shoulders.

Paul Meehan, an Indiana State Trooper and his wife, also a former police officer, along with their five kids all stood together. Meehan was a broad-shoul-dered, tough man whose calm demeanor had made him invaluable since they picked up him and his family just after Cincinnati.

James Ott, another Indiana State Trooper, and his wife and their three kids stood with them. The pair of them and their families had held out on the roof of a police station and James was a cheerful, hard worker. He'd been great at defusing conflicts between survivors and the cars the pair had guarded had some of the best rates of survivors getting along and doing what they were supposed to do.

There was Leah Paquette and her recon truck. The former firefighter and her crew had managed to survive in a firehouse in West Virginia. Several of them had died in Cincinnati, but the five survivors had stayed with him even after that disaster and they stood there now, with their families.

There had been others that he would have loved to have here. His friends, Robert Brockman and Tim Kennedy, and their families. Luis Cedano, the Professor, whose knowledge and analytical mind had helped to think through all manner of problems.

Dozens of others, too, for that matter, but he couldn't blame Josh Wachope for slipping away only with those he trusted to be quiet and do as they were told. Their former military, law enforcement, and emergency response personnel had been the train's reaction teams, the ones who fought off the undead and raiders, the ones that Jack had led into St. Louis to fight Nadal Malik's people.

It was a small number of people, and they couldn't leave the kids unprotected, either.

"Thank you, all of you," Jack told them, his throat choking up a bit as he said those words. They hadn't known if he was even going to survive, yet they had risked themselves and their families to come with Josh Wachope and slip him away from the train.

"We heard Fuller and Meelah on the radio," James Ott spoke up. "They're working together, it sounds like, and Meelah has Fuller switching over the tracks at Cuba to turn the train south."

"We have to stop them," Jack told them all. His mind went to the sensation of the threat, the *thing* that waited in the dark. "They're going into terrible danger."

***

Fuller gave a grin as the train trundled past the switch track in Cuba.

He frowned, though, as he counted trucks and noticed some missing. "Where's the Army trucks?"

Shamika had dropped off the side of the train as it rumbled past and she shouted over the sound of the train. "They pulled out, they took the Captain's body with them."

"He died?" Fuller asked in surprise. He had thought Captain Jack was one of the toughest people he'd ever met. Not like some kind of movie star tough, just *tough*. He'd seen the man wade into possessed with nothing more than that big knife of his.

"Meelah says he was dying," Shamika came up and she pulled his face down towards hers. Her hot breath on the side of his face got his blood pumping and the tongue she ran up the side of his cheek and into his ear made him forget any thoughts he had of the Captain.

"Damn, girl," He pushed her back a bit, "I'm workin'!"

She laughed, waving at the train as it rumbled past, people watching from the tops of some of the cars. "We don't need to work no more, Fuller. We *own* the train."

"Yeah..." Fuller grinned at her, though he felt a shiver of unease as he looked to the dense woods alongside the tracks... and the dead, overgrown town of Cuba.

*I fucking hate the forest,* he thought to himself. "Why not go to a town? That St James place could be nice, little small, but we could run that town, easy."

"Meelah says the woods will be better," Shamika told him.

"Meelah says a lot of shit," Fuller growled. He didn't like how Shamika had bought onto everything Meelah said. Shamika had been with the train and with Fuller for a while. Meelah had shown up just since the Captain had killed Malik, and now she was running things.

"Come on, babe, you're the muscle, she's the brains..." Shamika told him.

He didn't really like that, either. He was plenty smart, smart enough to run this whole thing. But he kept his mouth shut, because while he liked Shamika, he sure wasn't about to tell her that if he had the chance, he would dump a mag in Meelah 's back and leave her in the woods.

*Bitch would probably do it to me, too,* he told himself.

That was part of why he had his insurance, after all.

"Now that you have the train switched over," Shamika told him, "Meelah wants you to scout down the track, make sure it's clear."

"Ain't we got anyone else that can do that? I don't want to run into any devil plants," Fuller growled.

"No one else she trusts, Fuller," Shamika answered. "Now check it out, and quick, I want to spend the night with you, we got a whole car to ourselves. I pushed a bunch of those snot-nosed orphans to another car."

"Now *that* is good news," Fuller gave a whoop. He hopped back in his truck and slapped the dash. "Let's roll."

# Chapter Eleven

THE PRIESTESS KNELT, HER heart tremoring in her chest as she spoke. "Mistress, I have news."

"Of the ones who come?" The voice demanded. Emotion came in that voice, alien and terrible, and it inflicted physical pain on the priestess, even this far from the source.

"Yes, Mistress," The Priestess answered. "There are some among them that have taken over. They are leaderless and weak. They are coming south, coming closer."

The waters below stirred and surged in response. The Priestess could feel the ancient being below, feel her hunger. "Bring them to me."

"Yes, Mistress," The Priestess answered without hesitation.

She took that as a dismissal and stepped back from the platform, taking the stairs up and away from the tremendous underground lake and hurrying up, her feet moving rapidly despite the uneven steps and the dim light. She knew this path, had traveled it hundreds of times at this point.

She would have to figure out how to lead the survivors here, as a sacrifice to her god. She shuddered as she considered it. She had made sacrifices before, one and two people at a time, prisoners that she and her people had subdued and brought here.

She made those sacrifices to appease her god, and even as jaded as she was, the terrible screams and horrific noises that followed were not something that she enjoyed.

This was the only way to survive, in this world. To find some power greater than mere humans and to serve it, to worship it, no matter how awful it was. She understood that, just as she had understood to survive in the world before things were much the same.

She had no qualms about what she would do to the survivors. Certainly she didn't care, men, women, and children, about their lives. She went through the calculations on how to get them here, to further confuse them, to eliminate their leaders, and then to drive the unarmed civilians here for sacrifice to her Mistress.

As she reached the top, she had figured out what she would do and how she would do it.

It would be a long ride, their train could not come here, not to this terrible place, not directly. Their exiled leaders, though, they might...

As she came into the open, she touched her chest and the amulet, warm to the touch, that her Mistress had gifted her. At her finger's touch, she could feel a tremble of power as she sent out a call to the woods beyond the cave.

Forms shifted out of the dense trees around the cave entrance at her call. Servants of her god, mobile, carnivorous plants, the vine beasts that ambushed from hiding, the demon trees, which looked like twisted and blackened trees until they lurched into motion, and the last, the rotter, a towering mount that reeked of death, a tangle of vegetation taller than a building.

The last was the one that the Priestess had commanded to destroy holdouts of survivors here in her god's name, for when the other types could not suffice to eliminate them. Even gazing upon it made her head ache and the stench, even from fifty feet or more distance, had her fighting to keep from throwing up.

She sent them directions, pulsing the commands through her amulet. They had an alien intelligence of their own, unlike the mindless undead that some other, lesser, gods used. She could not be certain they fully understood her directions.

That was fine, they were only part of her plan. She had a long ride back to her people and from there, she needed to put her plan fully into action.

She would bring the train survivors here, to her god.

***

Captain Jack Zamora looked up as Tom Knighton stepped up in front of him carrying a large duffle bag.

"It is done," Knighton told him in an exhausted tone.

"What's done?" Jack frowned, not sure what his friend meant.

Knighton set the duffle bag down on the ground and unzipped it, revealing what looked like a bunch of curved metal plates. "I finished the forging back at the train. When Captain Wachope said it was time to go, I just had to bring it and my tools, I did the rest of the work in the time since. Thankfully I had already done a lot of it years ago and I'd brought it all with me. I hadn't known why until after you were injured."

"Tom, have you slept or eaten anything?" Jack asked, wondering if the man had snapped or driven himself past the point of mental coherence.

"I think I ate something, it doesn't matter. Anyway, it's done, you should try it on," Knighton told him.

"Try *what* on?" Jack asked.

Knighton showed him.

He laid it out, piece by piece, until it wasn't a collection of random metal plates, leather straps, and padding.

It was a suit of armor.

"Where the hell did you get chainmail, anyway?" Jack demanded, staring at the entire set.

"I made it, well, a long while back. Before all this. I hadn't made more, hadn't *felt* like making more, not until you got hurt, until I had a dream, that night, that it was time to make *this*." Knighton told him. "Put it on."

"Here?" Jack looked around, they were out in the open, in the shade of the trucks, while they got themselves ready to go take the train back.

"Where else?" Knighton asked. "I need to know it will fit right, and to make any necessary adjustments."

"I'll look..." He wanted to say absurd, but he didn't want to hurt his friend's feelings. He would, though, look ridiculous. Dressed up in armor... people would think he'd lost his mind.

"It will protect you, better than our standard body armor," Knighton told him. "Other than against bullets, but right now the threat isn't gunfire."

"It's going to be hot and restrictive," Jack protested.

"Not as restrictive as you think," Knighton shrugged, "Hot, though, yeah, it will be. Better than shattered ribs, though, right?"

Jack muttered something and reached forward to take the first piece. Getting it on was a process, he realized quickly as Knighton guided him through. It was like getting dressed, with layers on top of layers. The padding first, then the chainmail coat, then the armor, with each piece of that buckling on with straps, pulled tight over the chainmail.

Finally, there was the helmet, with the visor that he kept up for now, though that could drop down to protect his face.

He felt... surprisingly good. Jack twisted and stretched, impressed at both how well it fit and how agile he felt with all of it on. It *was* warm, the metal seemed absorb sunlight and Jack could feel sweat soaking him quickly in the Missouri summer heat. There was a weight to it, too, though felt far more distributed than his normal body armor.

"Now there," Captain Wachope came around the corner, "is sharp-dressed man."

Jack flushed, "Alright, dress time is over, help me get this off."

"Not a chance," Katie told him as she came up. "That's... you look *good*."

"I look absurd, people will think I've lost my mind," Jack protested. He reached up and unbuckled the chin strap and pulled the helmet off his head.

"Oof," Katie grinned, "My knight in shining armor."

She came up and leaned in for a kiss and Jack couldn't help but meet her.

"Ahem," Josh Wachope prompted them a moment later.

The kiss had gone on a bit longer than Jack had really planned, he pulled away reluctantly, dragging his attention away from Katie. "What, yes?"

"I came over to let you know, we have company. The lady from the town, uh..." Wachope frowned.

"Doctor Arden," Katie prompted him.

"Right, her, she's here with some of her people, they just rode up on horses, like they're out for a summer jaunt. Anyway, she's here, and wants to talk with you." Josh Wachope told him.

"Uh, let me get this off..." Jack began.

"She's *here,* might as well just talk to her as is," Wachope grinned, "even if it does look like you're about to ride out and slay a dragon."

"I think he looks hot," Katie grinned.

Jack didn't really know what to say in response to that, so he wisely kept his mouth shut.

He couldn't quite explain it, whether it was a physical thing or a mental one, but he did feel... *right* somehow in the armor.

They walked around the trucks, several of his people staring at him as he walked past.

Doctor Arden awaited them, with a cluster of her people. They were all tall, Jack noticed, which stood out to him, as did their long hair, many of them wearing it in braids similar to their leader.

He had no problem picking her out of the group. It was the way they all stood in relation to her, the way that she stood, it left no doubt. She was taller than most women, taller than several of the men, with auburn hair and leaf-green eyes.

There was a watchfulness to their expressions, a way that they stood, that told Jack they were on edge.

"I'm Captain Jack Zamora. Sorry I missed you before," Jack greeted her, "I'm just now up and around." He stepped forward and offered his hand, though she stared at it for a moment before extending her own and shaking.

"So, I see," Doctor Arden gave him a nod, her eyes narrowing as she took in the armor that he wore. "I had thought you were a Soldier, not a... historical reenactor?"

"One of my people made me this, I was just trying it on as you all came up," Jack told her. "I've served in the US Army, ten years, deployed to Iraq and Afghanistan."

"Interesting," Doctor Arden's tone left it open as to whether that was a good or bad thing.

"Look," Jack told her, "I'm pretty sure you didn't ride back out here to talk with us for no apparent reason. Something must have happened, between when you were out here talking with Captain Wachope, and when you came here. Something that's got your people on edge, clearly, and has put you questioning our presence, or else you wouldn't have shown up with an armed escort."

"You've quite the level of intuition," Doctor Arden noted.

"We should not trust them," One of her people suggested. "We can deal with this ourselves."

"We cannot, not without putting what we have preserved at risk," Arden answered over her shoulder. She faced Jack and cocked her head. "I assume your people have notified you about the military presence at Fort Leonard Wood?"

Jack gave her a nod, "They have."

"Do you work with them?" Arden asked.

"No," Jack answered her. Then, because she didn't look certain, he continued. "If it is the same Colonel Sinclair that I'm familiar with, he and I are unlikely to get along."

"Interesting, so you are no longer in service to the United States Army?" Arden raised an eyebrow.

"I'm in service to protecting the civilians from my train," Jack answered. "I still stand by the principles of the Army and the founding principles of the United States. That said, there's no government, we have no leadership, and my immediate priority is the safety and protection of my people."

"Then that may put you more at odds with Colonel Victor Sinclair than you even realize," Doctor Arden said in a grim tone. She went on, "My people called me back because Colonel Sinclair sent us a message. He wants all of our crops, our entire yield, including any seed corn we would need to grow crops next year."

"If you don't turn it over?" Jack figured he already knew the answer.

"Then he will take it, all of it, and the town as well," Doctor Arden said it with a sort of dread relish, as if it pleased her somehow to relay that information.

Jack opened his mouth to answer, as he did so, he heard distant sound, a sound so out of place that it took his mind several seconds to make sense of it. It was a small engine and it was *airborne*. He looked up and over and the others there did, as well.

Flying low, low enough that they clearly wanted it to be seen, came a military drone. *Shadow,* he noted, absently. He had no idea how they had one flying, still, where they had the fuel, the parts, or the rest of it.

The purpose of it was clear, though. They were checking out the town, watching what their leaders were doing.

And they knew about Jack and his group, now. Worse, they *wanted* them to know.

The drone swooped around in a loop and flew back towards the west, climbing and flying out of sight.

"Well," Jack said in a matter-of-fact tone. "That's going to be a problem."

# Chapter Twelve

"PULL UP THAT IMAGE again," Colonel Victor Sinclair ordered.

He squinted at the screen. "Who the hell is that loser?"

"Uh, I'm not sure, sir," His G2 answered. The officer sounded nervous, not that he shouldn't be, seeing as what had happened to his predecessor. *Man was trying to remove me, I did what needed to be done,* Sinclair thought absently.

"Can't we get a better image of his face?" Sinclair demanded. They stood in his command center. It had been an emergency operations center for the Engineer School, here at Fort Leonard Wood. It had taken his staff several months to get it just to his liking, with multiple displays, overlays, maps, and of course, the drone camera feed.

His staff officers and NCOs, too, were hard at work, many of them updating reports and running estimates for him on everything from their tactical situation to their reserves of fuel, ammunition, and food.

It was all powered, too, because Fort Leonard Wood not only had its own power plant, but it also had a variety of testbed power production equipment for the Engineer Prime Power school, some of which should allow them to keep the lights on for decades, with careful use.

"Sir, the sunlight is reflecting too much off his armor. I've got thermals, I've got lidar, but the glare off that shiny armor is too sharp a gradient with the angle of the imagery," Captain Riley answered.

He'd been *Lieutenant* Riley not all that long ago, before everything had crumbled. He'd followed Sinclair's orders, though, so he'd been field promoted.

Regulations allowed for that under unique situations and in Sinclair's perspective, this counted.

"Wish we had some Hellfires to drop on the bitch and whoever they are," Sinclair growled.

"Some of them look like they're military, sir," Captain Riley offered. It wasn't anything like an objection, he would never cross that line.

"Probably stolen or maybe weekend warriors," Sinclair snorted in disgust. "Army Reserve or National Guard, either way, it isn't likely that they are *proper* Soldiers." They had watched the progress of the train, off and on, ever since his geospatial technicians had noticed it crossing the Ohio River at Cincinnati. They hadn't been able to see much in the way of details of the survivors, though they certainly had not moved like any of the other surviving military groups.

Still, they did have three gun trucks, which itself was an accomplishment. It looked like they had gun mounts and ammunition for their weapons, too, which was also impressive, seeing as most military formations had burned through all their ammunition in a week or less of fighting the hordes of undead.

*And all the other horrible things out there,* Sinclair thought, his mind shying away from the terrible thoughts and images.

"Interesting that the locals went to meet them," Sinclair mused. He had shifted fairly early on to treating the entire situation like the insurgencies he had fought in Iraq and Afghanistan. He didn't think of the little surviving enclaves as citizens of the United States of America. They were locals. As such, they were either cooperative locals who did as he told or they were hostile locals who he would deal with as necessary.

He didn't yet have the manpower or trained leaders to move into them all and establish control, but that was where his recruitment and other plans would play towards, eventually. Colonel Sinclair had twenty-eight years of military service to draw upon, to apply the tools of war and diplomacy.

"Any issues bringing the bird back?" Colonel Sinclair asked.

"No, sir, landed without a problem," Captain Riley answered.

"Good, good," Sinclair nodded. The Shadow UAV was precious beyond belief at this point. Before all this, it had been a hundred-thousand dollar piece of equipment, for training operators to get their flight time in, before they reported to their units.

In that, it was like the vast majority of military equipment that Sinclair had. Fort Leonard Wood was one of the main training centers for not just the United States Army, but also for the Navy and Marine Corps, where they did combat engineer training, military police training, and chemical corps initial entry training for enlisted and officers.

He had one or two training sets for every bit of equipment they needed... and pretty much nothing more. It wasn't the kind of arsenal that he could reclaim the entire United States with... well, not yet, anyway.

Sinclair was a planner, though. And among the various things he *did* have was access to the National Reconnaissance Office's satellites via a direct connection at the geospatial lab. He had satellite imagery of the entire country. With that access, Sinclair could see where armor and equipment lay abandoned across the country. He had identified where enclaves of people held out...

*And where terrible things that shouldn't exist somehow... do.* Again, his mind shied away from that thought, though. He knew just how dangerous it was to spend too much time looking at some of that imagery, especially places, like in China, where the very worst of the worst had occurred.

In the immediate aftermath, the geospatial staff had suffered the worst of casualties, many of them self-inflicted as men and women had gone mad looking at some of the things, impossible, *terrible* things that had sprung into existence across the globe.

Portals to hell, some had called them, even as they clawed their eyes with their own fingernails.

That hadn't stopped Colonel Sinclair from continuing the work. A few lives lost would pay vast dividends. There were entire formations of armor and stockpiles of ammunition and fuel waiting for him. With careful planning, judicious use, and the slow, steady establishment of control, he knew he could restore order. *His* order.

"Do we know why the train turned south?" Colonel Sinclair asked.

"No, sir, not yet," Captain Riley answered. "It could be they got some intel from the locals..."

"No one goes in there and comes back out," Colonel Sinclair shook his head. Then again, he had said much the same about St. Louis, only a month earlier when Captain Riley had reported the train full of survivors headed there. They didn't know *exactly* what had transpired, the satellites hadn't been overhead when it had gone down, but the would-be warlord who had controlled the town did not appear to have come out of it, and the train had continued on its way.

*And the entire northern end of the city is torn up from explosions and fires,* Colonel Sinclair reminded himself.

"Keep an eye on them, and on the train," Colonel Sinclair ordered. "Let me know immediately if there are any changes."

"Yes, sir," Captain Riley nodded.

Sinclair looked at his watch and considered the time. "My wife is hosting another social this evening. Be there, dress uniform, of course." He paused and considered his subordinate. "Are you bringing the young blonde one, again?"

"Nichel?" Captain Riley asked.

"Yeah, the local girl, right?" Sinclair asked.

Captain Riley nodded.

"Don't bring her, the wife didn't like her," Sinclair ordered. "She dressed too trashy."

"Of course, sir," Captain Riley nodded. As one of his senior officers, he could ask just about any woman to accompany him to one of Colonel Sinclair's socials. Much to Sinclair's amusement, Riley had used that to his advantage, showing up with all manner of beautiful ladies. Not that Riley wouldn't have been able to get them otherwise, Sinclair knew. He was a handsome, charming man. Still, the knowledge that he was powerful, that he was important, certainly gave him an advantage.

*Good for him,* Colonel Sinclair thought. The young man *should* have his pick of women. Maybe he would even be fortunate enough to find a woman as good as his own wife.

"Nineteen hundred, sharp," Sinclair reminded him. Then he turned away, striding out of the command center.

His mind, though, wandered back to the figure in armor. Who was he? Why did not being able to see the man's face bother him so?

***

"What do we do?" Captain Josh Wachope asked.

They had moved back from Doctor Arden and her group to discuss things.

Jack really didn't like the situation. Having an Unmanned Aerial Vehicle was a significant advantage to any military force. Colonel Sinclair's people would be able to see his people moving, see where they were going, and potentially move a force in to oppose them.

Back on the train a few of their scout trucks had some simple quad-copters, but the batteries and parts only lasted so long and they only had so much range.

That Shadow, and anything else they might have, would give Colonel Sinclair's people a tremendous advantage. Sure, it couldn't be up all the time and there would have to be limitations on parts and fuel, but it was still a significant threat.

"Did she say how many people Colonel Sinclair has?" Jack asked, his gaze going to the dense trees and hills to the west.

"She didn't, but from the way they're acting, it's more than a handful," Captain Wachope frowned. "I mean, the installation had several thousand people, it wasn't exactly a *small* post."

109

There were Military Police, Chemical, Transportation, and Engineer units assigned there, as well as the school-houses for those branches. Their assumption, up until recently, was that the installation's forces had met the same, unfortunate, fate as most of the US Military, that they had rolled out to support the defense against the rising threat of the undead and that they had succumbed as they ran out of ammunition and fuel.

Some part of Jack had hoped they might find some military survivors. Knowing that they were led by the same asshole that had ended his career left him feeling betrayed.

"We need to find out more, find out what they have, who they have," Jack mused. "We need to get over and stop the train." He felt in his bones that they needed to do that, first. The threat, though, of whatever forces Colonel Sinclair had, could not be ignored.

"There's the raiders, too, up at St James," Josh warned.

"I know, we have a myriad of problems and only so many people," Jack started to run a hand over his face, realized he still wore chainmail gloves and gauntlets, and settled for cracking his neck instead.

They had six trucks: Brian Gnad's rail truck and the three gun trucks, plus two more recon trucks that had come with them. They had more people than they really should move in those vehicles. They also had their dependents, the families of those who had come, so that they wouldn't be at risk back on the train.

Four problems, six trucks. He couldn't leave enough trucks here to defend their people, he couldn't split them out in four different directions, either.

His gaze went to where Doctor Arden and her people stood talking. He could well imagine their discussion, how they should be back in their town, making preparations.

They couldn't fight Colonel Sinclair, either. Not with the assets he might have, not until they knew more about what he *did* have.

"With his drone up, we have no way to get close and figure out what Colonel Sinclair has," Jack mused.

"Not with our trucks anyway," Josh Wachope snorted, "and given the hostility of the plant-life thus far, I certainly am not about to send anyone on foot, either; especially not when the Shadow probably has thermals that could pick them up through the trees anyway."

*Unless...*

"What if we don't try to sneak in to see what he has?" Jack asked out loud.

"I'm not following," Josh Wachope frowned.

"What about sending the three trucks straight in, waving hello, playing friendly?" Jack asked.

"He knows you, and from what you told me, he's not particularly fond of you," Josh cautioned.

"Yeah... but he doesn't know *you*... He doesn't, hopefully, know I'm even here." Jack began to feel a plan coming together.

"We have the train to worry about and —"

"I can handle the train," Jack felt confidence seep in even as he said it. "Look, you can take the gun trucks, get in, figure out what is going on, and get back out."

"Because that worked out so well for *you* in St. Louis," Wachope shook his head.

"Maybe not, but you'll have more resources and..."

"And Sinclair already knows we're working with the locals, he's got the drone, and we've got families with us," There was a note of genuine fear in his friend's voice.

"Yeah, and I am suggesting *they* go with Leah and the other two recon trucks to Rolla with Arden and her people," Jack told him. "They can hide out with them while you figure out what's going on at Fort Lost-in-the-Woods and I get our train going the right direction."

Josh Wachope looked conflicted, "We barely met these people, you want me to trust our families with them?"

"We have to trust someone," Jack answered, "and right now, we have common enemies."

"What if they're manipulating us to get us to fight Sinclair for them?" Josh asked. "They could use our families as hostages."

Jack gave him a level look, "Josh, we're in a position right now where no matter what we do, we've got problems. There's evil plants, raiders, someone's hijacked our train and there's a potentially power-crazed military officer to deal with. We can show these people," Jack waved at where Doctor Arden and her people stood, "that we trust them and that they can work with us, maybe make them allies. I go get the train back, and you figure out what resources Sinclair has."

"And if something goes wrong?" Josh asked in a low voice. "If Sinclair attacks Rolla while my wife and kids are there?"

"Then you stop him," Jack told him in a hard voice. "You stop him, just like I know you would, anyway, because you're not about to let some power-tripping asshole kill a bunch of people."

His friend looked down, "Alright. I think it goes without saying, but I don't like this plan."

"I haven't liked *any* plan we've had since this began," Jack told him. He had never really believed that Paul would have fixed the train, he had assumed that they were all as good as dead from the beginning. He just didn't have it in him to give up.

***

"Why do I gotta go with him, again?" Sean McCune asked in an irritated tone. He was worried about Sandra and her kids. For maybe the first time in his life, there was someone he cared about more than himself, and now they were sending him in the opposite direction.

"Because, if there's something shady going on, you're the best person we have to find out what it is," Captain Zamora told him.

"I *am* good at that," Sean nodded despite himself.

"Exactly, shady is what you do," Captain Zamora nodded.

"Hey..." Sean's eyes narrowed, but the Captain had already turned away to other things.

"Hey buddy, you're looking sharp," Larry Southard slapped him on the shoulder.

Sean glowered at his friend in suspicion, "What do you mean by that, exactly?"

"The military duds, funny they had a uniform that fit you, huh?" Larry asked.

"Ah, I found this a couple months back," Sean told him. "Mostly my size, so it works."

That was how they had picked him over Larry for this, he figured. Infiltrating a bunch of military survivors, Sean could at least look the part, though he hoped they didn't expect him to salute or any of that crap.

"You need a trim, hair and face," Larry grinned.

"I ain't gonna do that," Sean protested. "Not a one of even the proper Army soldiers does that anymore." Razor blades were hard to find, shaving cream didn't exist, and they didn't have electric trimmers or anything.

"The Captain does," Larry grinned as he ran a hand over his own beard. "Has a straight blade razor, takes a steady hand to do that."

Sean's gaze went to where their leader stood, still wearing the polished steel armor, still looking like a knight out of some fairy tale. "Yeah," Sean nodded, "Sure does."

***

"You are going to get your people, from the deep woods?" Doctor Arden walked up as Jack finished checking his gear. He still wore the new armor, feeling self-conscious about it but not enough to take it off.

The heat and humidity had him sweating rather more than he liked, though, and he had been drinking a ton of water.

"Yes," Jack gave her a nod. "I want to say, as well, thank you for taking our families in while I take care of this."

She gave a slight wave of her hand, "That is nothing. Be very careful, going in there."

"You've... seen some of the things there?" Jack asked. He wasn't sure he felt comfortable talking about man-eating plants. It seemed a little crazy. *The whole world is crazy.*

"We have scouted the edges of the forest and there are a handful of survivors who have escaped," The professor clasped her hands in an almost religious pose. "The things there, they are ancient, primeval."

"How would you know?" Jack asked with narrowed eyes. After how Nidal Malik had worked with the nightwalker, he wasn't about to rule out someone else working with such things.

"Plants with rapid vascular movement, like a venus fly trap or bladderwort. Plants that release spores, like ferns or fungi, like the first plants that grew across the early planet," she told him.

"Spores?" Jack asked with a frown. He didn't like the sound of that.

"Some of the survivors, they spoke of a green fog that rises in the depths of the woods. Anyone who goes inside it is affected. It makes it hard to breathe, hard to see, and triggers allergic reactions. It precedes the most dangerous attacks."

Jack made a mental note to see if they had any gas masks in their gear. He thought they had a few stashed away. Even so, the filters only lasted so long, and who knew if they would be effective against something like this?

"Why do you say ancient?" Jack asked.

"Reproduction through spores is part of the first land plants, before there was animal life to facilitate pollination," Doctor Arden answered. "My theory is that these plants lay dormant, maybe even just their spores, and whatever happened in the world with the possessed, they woke up."

"So these ancient plants just woke up and started murdering people?" Jack asked dubiously. "The same time that we have possessed undead running around and demonic nightwalkers?"

She shrugged, "I don't know, maybe they're aliens from outer space, maybe they are more of these demonic things like this 'nightwalker' you mentioned. My theory is that they are different."

"Either way, I've got to deal with them," Jack nodded. "Any tips?"

"Don't trust anything in there," She pointed at the dark woods. "All the survivors who escaped and those of our scouts who have been there can all confirm, there is something deeply wrong with the plants there; not just the ones actively trying to kill you. Stick to the road surface and don't trust any trails. Don't trust any noises you hear."

"Anything else?" Jack nodded.

"If you see a green fog rising, get out of there," Doctor Arden told him. She gave him a last nod, almost a benediction, "May you be blessed."

She turned and walked back to her group.

***

"I don't like this," Katie stared at Jack, her eyes locked on his face.

She couldn't say if she was trying to memorize his features in case of the worst or to try and gauge the impact of her words. Maybe it was a little of both.

Jack looked over at her, his expression somber. "It doesn't matter what we like, it matters what we need to do. I need to go get the train turned around. Josh needs to go and find out what Colonel Sinclair is up to, and you…"

"I need to take the 'womenfolk and chillins' to safety?" Katie asked in an acerbic tone.

He gave her a level look. "You can manage them, keep an eye on Doctor Arden and her group, and most importantly, I *trust* you. Leah Paquette is there to back you up, her firefighters can be the muscle to get you out, but I trust *your* judgement."

"I don't want to be left behind, and I can't help but think it's because —"

"It's because I trust *you* more than anyone to keep the rest of them safe," Jack told her. "That's it. Believe me, if I could, I'd have you with me the whole way, every minute, every second. I'm not sending you away for your safety. I'm sending you to watch over *them*. Because there is no one I trust to do it better."

Katie's eyes teared up and she stepped forward. Embracing him, she could feel the cold hard edges of his armor, and it felt to her like they were more than physical things. Jack armored himself and others from the world and it made for hard choices and hard edges.

Just like the armor, though, she knew there was a core of compassion underneath.

"Be safe," Katie told him.

"I'll be fine," Jack assured her. He gave her a gentle squeeze and then, just as gently, pried her arms loose and stepped back. "I'll see you in a day or two, I promise."

He turned and walked towards Brian Gnad's truck and he didn't look back.

# Chapter Thirteen

"WHAT THE HELL IS that?" Fuller snapped.

"Dunno, I don't like this shit," That came from Dennis, his driver. Dennis knew how to drive anything, which was why Fuller had him as his driver. Dennis had been boosting cars from when he was thirteen.

Fuller stared ahead through the dense fog, which had a green look to it, and at how the tracks terminated in a tangle of vines and vegetation. It was as if the tracks just ended, and with the way the trees loomed in at them from all sides, it gave Fuller a bad feeling about all this.

"Terrence, Sherrick, get your asses out there and see if we can clear the tracks," Fuller ordered.

"Fuller, I don't like this," Terrence whined.

"Get your coward ass out there," Sherrick ordered, shoving Terrence out the door before climbing out himself. Sherrick was a big dude, he had been Fuller's second for a decade, now. He was big enough he might have made it in professional football, fast enough, too.

His temper had flushed all that down the toilet, Fuller knew. Sherrick's temper had gotten him thrown off any team he played. Fuller had once seen him grab a coach and slam the man's head in the locker room door seven times because they'd lost a game. The only way Fuller kept him in line was playing his anger and irritation off on other members of his crew.

And, since he had ordered Sherrick out, he had to show that he wasn't a coward, too, otherwise Sherrick might start thinking about being number one.

The air outside the truck was hot, thick, and heavy. There was dense fog rising, with a greenish tint to it that he didn't like. Fuller coughed a bit, the fog irritating his throat.

He pulled his machete out, and the other pair had their blades ready as well. Terrence had a normal machete, a cheap blade they'd looted from a sporting goods store.

Sherrick had a huge forward curved blade. He had hacked possessed to pieces with that thing, and Fuller had seen him do the same to any survivors who had stuff they wanted, before they met up with the train and went straight. *Well, mostly straight.*

Even though it was early afternoon, the fog and trees made it seem like dusk, and Terrence had his flashlight, one of the stupid shake to power ones that they'd found at the same sporting goods place. It worked well enough, but he looked like an idiot as he shook it up and down to charge it.

It made a lot of noise, too, which made Fuller realize how quiet it had gone. There weren't any birds or bugs or anything. The only noise was the truck behind them and the thunk-slide of the shake light.

"Is that a fallen tree or just vines or is there a train car in there?" Fuller asked impatiently.

Terrence shone his light on the tangle of vines and stuff, "I don't know, Fuller."

"Well, get in there and start cutting the shit off," Fuller snapped.

"But there's... things," Terrence whined.

"Get your ass movin," Sherrick gave the man a shove and followed after.

Evidently his fear of rumored murderous plants was a lot less than his terror of the confirmed murderous Sherrick. Terrence started clearing vines, hacking at them and pulling them away, juggling his flashlight and sending light in swooping arcs around them.

The fog seemed to be getting thicker and Fuller coughed again, feeling snot dripping down like he had hay fever or something. His eyes were getting irritated too, and he wiped at them and coughed and spat.

"Doesn't look like there's anything here, just vines," Sherrick called.

"Some of these are really thick, I —"

Terrence's words cut off and there was a thud, followed shortly by a clatter as his flashlight hit the ground.

"What the fuck?" Fuller spun, looking at where the man had been standing. There was no sign of him on the tracks, just his flashlight.

Sherrick swung his big blade around, slicing through the vines around him, but nothing moved.

"Dennis, you see anything?" Fuller shouted back at the truck, not taking his eyes off the vines where Terrence had disappeared.

Sherrick had moved forward, snagging the flashlight and backed up again, swinging his big blade around menacingly.

"Dennis!" Fuller snapped. "What the hell, man?" He backed up to the truck, squinting against the headlights, and then went around to the driver side door.

The door was open. Dennis was nowhere to be seen.

"Oh, fuck this," Fuller coughed again, this time his chest hurting as he did so. He wiped again at his running nose, and this time his hand came away with a smear of blood.

"Sherrick, get your ass back here, fuck this shit," Fuller climbed into the driver's seat and pulled the door closed.

His second turned towards the truck, and that was when Fuller saw it. It wasn't the vines on the ground; it was the fucking *trees*. Looming above them, a long, powerful limb swung down at Sherrick. The big man saw it coming, somehow, and rolled to the side.

"Fucking *run* man!" Fuller called.

Sherrick either didn't hear him or his temper had taken over. The big man took his big blade in two hands and ran at the thing. He swung the blade right into one of the trunk-like legs of the tree monster and the steel bit deep, almost driving through it.

The tree thing swung in return, though. Claw-like branches ripped through him, and blood spattered the truck's windshield in enough quantity that Fuller knew better than to worry if Sherrick was still alive and needed help.

He put the truck in reverse and slammed the gas pedal. The truck bounced and bobbed on the tracks. Fuller couldn't see, the front windshield was blood and fog and the reverse lights barely illuminated anything behind him.

The back end of the truck hit something and the steering wheel jerked in his hands. The front end of the truck swung around and then the truck was driving down the side of the rail embankment and slammed into a tree.

The impact was enough to bounce Fuller almost out of the seat. He fumbled with the gear shifter, his hands shaking so much he could barely get them to work.

Something loomed above him, silhouetted in the headlights, barely visible with the blood on the windscreen. Fuller screamed, fighting to shift the truck into drive.

He was still screaming as a huge arm punched through the windshield and grabbed him around the chest and ripped him out of the seat.

***

"Where is that moron?" Meelah snapped. Fuller was supposed to be back by now. She had sent him ahead to do the final stretch of tracks; it shouldn't have taken him *this* long just to do the last bit to Virbinium.

"Probably found a piece of ass," Shamika laughed.

Meelah shot the woman a glare. "I thought I told you to keep him happy in that regard?"

"I did," Shamika answered defensively, "that doesn't mean he's not likely to chase more of it if there's the opportunity. He's insatiable."

Meelah had put the woman to keeping Fuller happy and distracted. If he was both of those things, he was less likely to cause problems with her being in charge.

"I don't like that he's late," Meelah grumbled. They had stopped the train, which she *also* didn't like. With it stopped, people talked, they had time to think, and the quiet of the woods around them was ominous and threatening.

She wanted them afraid, yes, but with the train stopped, they thought about *options*, such as backing off this dead-end track and going somewhere else.

Meelah couldn't let that happen. She had spent the last night tossing and turning from nightmares. The tattoo on her chest had begun to burn, a cold, painful sensation that had made true sleep impossible. Every time she had dozed off, there had been more of the nightmares. A terrible, armor-clad knight that chased her through her dreams. Yet as she ran from him, there was only one place she could go... back into the arms of *Meslamtaeda*.

Her merely human mind recoiled even as she thought of the name of Nidal Malik's god. The tattoo between her breasts pulsed in time to her thoughts, though, the cold burn leaching into her flesh.

She found her hands trembling, her mind flittering away from the thought. The god she had sworn herself to, thinking it was just some superstition, the god that had gifted Nidal Malik incredible power.

She didn't know if the nightmare was something brought on by stress, if it was some kind of warning, or if the god that she had abandoned had decided it was not done with her.

"Thayvan," Meelah snapped, "Go get on the radio, see where that idiot is."

"Uh, sure thing," Thayvan nodded. The big, somewhat simple, man hurried over to the radio set. She probably should have put someone smarter on the task, possibly even Shamika, but right now, she wanted someone she trusted to do it.

With how unconcerned Shamika seemed, Meelah wasn't sure she could trust the woman.

"Marrik, how are things in the rest of the train?" Meelah asked sharply.

Marrik looked up, his expression wary. "There's people starting to ask questions." She had recruited him from back when they had both been servants to Nadal Malik. He spoke with a harsh rasp, the product of a scar that ran across his neck. He told people that someone had tried to kill him and he'd killed them instead.

"What sort of questions?" Meelah demanded. She wasn't impressed or afraid of that scar or his rasp. When she had earned his trust, he had admitted he was in a car accident, driving drunk, he'd killed a family of three. The police on the scene had saved his life, and he would have gone to jail for life, save that the end of the world had intervened before his trial.

"Like why we've moved everyone around, why you have a car to yourself, that sort of thing," Marrik rasped back. He was a big man, physically-imposing, and she appreciated that he knew how to use his size to his advantage.

"Did you make examples of the ones who asked?" Meelah snapped.

"I beat up a few of them," He shrugged. "They're still asking the questions, asking what happened with the Captain, too."

"He's dead," Meelah snapped. "Make sure they understand that."

"We don't have no body," Shamika sassed.

Meelah shot her a glare, "Whose fault is that?"

Shamika flushed. She'd been assigned to watch for anyone trying to sneak away, but in the rapid change of power after the 'vote' that Meelah had rigged with promises and favors, she hadn't noticed the Soldiers leaving with their gun trucks and the Captain's body.

That had been the plan, of course. Sooner or later, their leader's run of luck would run out, he would end up injured or dead, and then Meelah would engineer a vote and seize power. She hadn't expected it to happen quite so soon, of course. She hadn't had as many people lined up to help her run things and she wasn't sure exactly who she could trust.

That was one reason she sent Fuller ahead to scout, because she figured he would back her on this move, as long as she kept him happy, anyway.

"They aren't answering the radio," Thayvan told her.

"Try again," Meelah snapped at him.

Her gaze went to Marrik and Shamika. "Who are the ones causing the most trouble?"

"The friends of the Captain," Marrik told her. "Cedano, Kennedy, Brockman, a few others."

Of course it was. They were some of the most necessary people, too, the ones with the skills and knowledge about how the train functioned, and their families. If she hurt them, at least right now while she still needed the train, she risked not being able to get it going once more.

"What about the scout trucks?" Meelah demanded. That had been something she had done immediately after they noticed the soldiers gone. She had taken the keys to all the trucks; no one was going anywhere without her say-so.

They had also taken over the armory with most of the remaining guns. Many of the other survivors on the train still had some and almost all of the adults had knives and even axes or spears for fending off possessed. Still, her people had most of the guns and the ammunition supply, as well.

"No one has been near them, our people are watching," Marrik assured her.

She didn't really want to send any of her people on those trucks. Scouting was dangerous business, Fuller and his team were experienced at it. They weren't the best, but they were good enough. She didn't want to thin out her numbers sending out scouts and risking her people. She couldn't risk the normal scouts deciding to cut their losses, either.

"Huh, that's funny," Thayvan said from up front, by the radio.

"What's funny?" Meelah asked in a tone of irritation. "Did you get Fuller on the radio?"

"Uh, no," Thayvan answered. "It's just getting really dark outside, and it's not even that late."

123

"What?" Meelah moved to the front of the engine cab and looked out the windows. Sure enough, the sky had begun to darken and there was a thick fog rising. It had a distinct greenish tinge to it, as well, as it seeped out of the trees.

Meelah felt uncertainty tremor through her. There was something menacing about that fog.

"Ignore the fog," Meelah snapped. "Get that idiot Fuller on the radio."

She turned back to Marrik and Shamika, "You two, go make sure our people are alert, I don't want anyone getting any ideas about slipping away in this fog."

"What about..." Shamika began.

"I told you to move," Meelah snapped.

They hurried out.

For her part, Meelah went to the windows and stared south, south where she felt called. The tattoo on her chest itched and burned and she scratched at it, her nails sharp on her flesh.

***

"Here we go," Jack muttered as the road dove into the dense trees. Vines hung down from above and even grew over the road in places.

Brian drove onward without a word, though Jack could see the other man's knuckles were white on his steering wheel.

Jack didn't have his normal party with him; he'd sent Lieutenant Baxter and Warrant Officer Knighton with Josh Wachope. Larry sat in the back seat, along with Paul Meehan and James Ott, the pair of former State Troopers had riot guns and pistols, along with the ubiquitous long blade that most of them carried for possessed defense. Meehan had a fire axe and James Ott had a double-headed wood-cutting axe.

Even as he thought that, forms appeared in the road in front of the truck.

"Crap," Brian muttered.

"There's only a few of them, we can clear them out of the way and move on," Paul Meehan said from the back seat.

Jack wasn't as sure about it, but they had to clear the possessed out of the road, they couldn't risk one of them damaging the truck. Worse would be if they bogged the truck down so they got stuck.

"Paul and James, with me, Larry and Brian, watch our backs," Jack ordered.

Brian stopped the truck and the three of them bailed out. Jack drew his blade even as the first of the possessed lurched toward him.

The eighteen-inch blade had a broad cutting head and Jack advanced on the possessed, backlit by the truck's headlights.

Jack noticed differences from the normal possessed that he'd dealt with. These had growths all over their bodies, pushing through their ragged clothing and gray skin.

He went in at them with the tempered aggression that had served him well enough before. The first thing he did was drive his chopping blade down on the shoulder socket of the nearest possessed.

That was when he realized that things were not going well.

Instead of driving through the shoulder and disabling the limb, the blade only bit in, as if the flesh were far denser. The possessed immediately lashed at him, with both whole arms, and Jack pulled back, tugging hard to try and pull his blade free. It was caught, though, and he just pulled the possessed with him.

"What the hell?" Paul shouted.

Jack kicked his possessed, hard, in the chest, knocking it back and freeing his weapon. He spared a glance. Paul Meehan had severed a possessed's arm with his fire axe. But the possessed had stopped and picked up its limb. As they watched, the possessed lifted the severed limb and tendrils grew out from each severed end, connecting it back on.

Jack's possessed had got back up, the kick that should have shattered its ribs and at least slowed it had only knocked it down.

"I got this!" Larry shouted and Jack heard the whine of the electric chain saw. Larry gave a whoop as he ran forward. He shoulder checked the nearest possessed, driving it to the ground and hitting it with the chainsaw. Jack stepped forward, helping to keep the possessed down.

"This is taking too long," Jack shouted.

Indeed, coming out of the woods, he saw several more of the possessed.

"Got this one," Larry panted, kicking the severed head away and then chucking a leg in the other direction.

"Get it off me!" James Ott shouted. Jack spun, seeing that a possessed had tackled the former state trooper to the ground. As Jack ran forward to help, the undead's jaws open and a cloud of green billowed from its mouth and across James' face.

Jack shifted his sprint into a kick, hitting the possessed in the hip in a blow that he felt all the way up his spine. The undead tumbled away and Jack pulled the coughing trooper back to his feet.

"Next one's down!" Larry called excitedly.

"Uh, we got a problem," Paul Meehan shouted. "We've got a *really* big problem."

It was another of the demonic trees and it lumbered forward out of the fog, more possessed following in its wake.

"Brian, you're up!" Jack called.

"You sure?" Brian asked from the truck.

"Just do it!" Jack panted as they backed away from the approaching possessed.

"This didn't work in Cincinnati..."

"Just fucking hit them!" Jack bellowed.

From the truck, there was a snap and a hiss as Brian lit the igniter.

A moment later, he fired the flamethrower.

The wash of heat was indescribable. The hot, humid day became far hotter. Yellow fire lit up the murky day and billowing flames and smoke rose up from where that fire touched.

All of the plant-infested possessed froze, or at least, the ones that weren't on fire. The looming demonic tree froze as well.

"Get some!" Brian shouted eagerly. "You all don't like bubba's little flamethrower, do ya?"

The older man giggled, "Bubba's truck has a flamethrower and it's coming for you!"

He washed the fire across the lead possessed and the ones it ignited, thrashed and fled, trailing fire into the trees. Everything was too wet to get a good blaze going, but they still trailed droplets of fire as they fled.

Jack and the others backed to the truck as Brian washed fire across the lead possessed again, the gout of flame going forty feet or more. When he hit the tree was when things *really* got crazy.

The tree, similar to the one that Jack had hit with thermite, went up like it was made of pitch.

It thrashed, fire engulfing it. Huge burning limbs swung through the possessed around it, crushing them, setting some afire, and then the huge thing fell, thrashing and burning on the ground, knocking over and setting trees and brush afire, crushing possessed, and making the ground tremble in its demise.

The infested possessed burned like candles, the vine growths running through their flesh ignited as easily as the tree.

"I'm out," Brian called.

"Man, I wish I had some marshmallows," Larry chortled. "We could make s'mores."

The tree kept thrashing until long after an animal would have stopped moving. Burning limbs twitched and thrashed until they crumbled to ash. The possessed had burned down at that point as well, until there was nothing left besides charred remnants.

The forest, already still, had gone ominously quiet.

"Uh... I think we should get in the truck," Larry's goofy smile grew a bit brittle.

The trees seemed to loom over them. The green fog had burned off, replaced by smoke... but a new bank of fog rose up, denser than before, a rolling bank that came through the trees like a slow-cresting wave.

"Get in the truck, move!" Jack snapped.

They piled in, and even before Jack was fully into the vehicle, Brian hit the gas.

The wall of green fog continued to roll towards them, caught by the edges of Brian's headlights. Larry reached forward and messed with the rotating flood lights on Brian's control panel, swiveling them around to shine on the bank of green fog.

"There's... *things* moving in there," Larry said with a worried gulp.

Something in that bank of fog hit a tree under the shine of the light and the tree toppled in their direction, Brian gunned the engine and it slammed into the ground behind them.

"*Big* things," Larry shuddered.

"Drive faster," Jack ordered.

"This isn't exactly Talladega Speedway," Brian ground out as the road twisted and turned through the woods and hills.

Jack watched out the side and through the rear-view mirror. They were drawing ahead of the fog, but it didn't need to follow the road and even as they wound away from it now, the road curved back towards it. Larry swung the floods back in that direction.

"Larry, stop fiddling with the lights and pull up our map, if we miss a turn, we're as good as dead," Jack snapped.

"James is not doing so good," Paul spoke from the back.

"What do you mean?" Jack asked.

"Left in, uh... a quarter mile, I think," Larry squinted at the map.

James had begun to cough. Jack turned in his seat, looking at the former state trooper. James's skin had gone gray and he was coughing, great wracking coughs as he tried to get that green stuff out of his lungs.

Only it wasn't green stuff that came out. There was black stuff. And flecks of blood that spattered his window.

"I can't, I can't get my breath," James gasped and coughed again.

"James," Jack snapped, "Stay with us. Take a deep breath."

"I…" He bent double, coughing again, and this time he hacked out a spiky-looking object almost the size of a quarter. Larry turned his flashlight on it and Jack, looking down at the floorboard, saw the thing *writhe* in the light.

"Holy shit, what's that?" Larry asked.

The thing continued to wriggle, the spines on it had hooks and bits of meat and blood glistened on them. Jack's stomach rolled over, "Get a jar or something, grab it."

Paul Meehan reached over, snagging the thing in a glass salsa jar and closing the lid on it.

James Ott gave a wet sounding groan and then slumped over in his seat.

"Check him," Jack ordered. If he'd died, they had no choice but to dump the body. Otherwise, he would rise as a possessed undead… or worse, one of those awful plant things.

Larry reached out and checked the man's pulse. He looked at Jack and shook his head.

"Shit," Jack shook his head. The thing back there hadn't done anything but *breathe* on him.

"Oh, there's the turn," Larry said helpfully.

"Stop here," Jack ordered.

Brian skidded to a halt.

Paul reached over and opened James's door.

Larry did the honors, dumping James's body out on the road. Normally they'd do the decent thing and chop him up. They didn't have time, though. The fog continued to roll towards them, fifty yards or less away.

Larry pulled the door shut and Brian accelerated away. In the side mirror, Jack saw the limp figure they'd left in the road. He'd failed the man. Jack would have to explain to the man's wife and kids. He would have to tell them what had happened and why.

He prayed that it would be worth it.

As they drove, it began to rain again, big, heavy drops that thundered on the truck's roof.

# Chapter Fourteen

"Shamika," Meelah snapped, "Where is Fuller?"

The other woman looked up from rolling a joint. Meelah wasn't sure where she had found the stash. She hadn't asked or really cared. Presumably she'd either had it already, or, more likely, taken it from some of the other survivors on the train.

"I don't know," Shamika's hands trembled a little bit as she tried to roll the paper, her fingers trembling with fear.

Meelah despised that weakness.

"Get out there and find him," Meelah ordered.

"Out *there*?" Shamika gestured at the dense rain and fog that lay outside of the engine's crew cab. As if to punctuate her words, green lightning flared, illuminating the tracks and train for a moment in a surreal fashion.

Meelah stood up, "Yes, out there you silly twit. I need Fuller and his thugs. Go find them."

Shamika looked between the heavy rain outside and back at Meelah.

"Thayvan, Marrik," Meelah's voice shifted to a more moderate tone.

"Ma'am?" The two men rose from where they had sat to either side of her.

"I think Miss Shamika needs a reminder of who is in charge," Meelah smiled.

Shamika threw down her weed and backed to the door, "I'm going, I'm going."

"Watch her," Meelah ordered. She didn't trust the other woman. She seemed too unconcerned about Fuller's disappearance.

The rain thundered down, the fat drops causing a roar even in the soundproofed cab. Shamika was soaked to the skin within seconds and the woman staggered through the rain towards the trucks.

"She forgot to get keys," Marrik noted.

"Good," Meelah sneered. She wanted the woman humbled. They'd been stationary too long. Whether Fuller came back or not, she was going to order the train forward. This was Shamika's fault; she should have kept a better leash on Fuller.

The idiot had probably been distracted by something and gone off to loot or steal. He was short-sighted, all her people were. They didn't know, they couldn't know, that this wasn't about mere humans.

She could feel it in her bones. The rain wasn't natural; this was sent by the thing that lurked in the woods. The god or demon that had caused fear in Nidal Malik. *I will find it, I will appease it, and...*

"Hey, I see lights," Trayvan called.

Meelah moved to the window, frowning as she made out the bright lights even through the downpour. The lights approached from the side, not down the tracks from the direction she had sent Fuller. For that matter, the truck lights seemed brighter than Fuller's truck, too.

"Where did Shamika go?" Marrik rasped.

He wasn't wrong; the woman, stumbling towards the parked trucks, had vanished.

"She was moving through the brush there," Trayvan pointed helpfully. "Oh, I think I see her, she's just tangled up."

"It's a trap, it has to be," Meelah snapped. "Get our weapons, Fuller's back to attack and take the train, Shamika's working with him. Sound the alert, warn our people."

Marrik grabbed a rifle and his hatchet and rushed out. Trayvan stood there, his expression blank, clearly not sure what to do.

*Simple minded, useful at times, less so at others, Meelah* sighed to herself. "Kill the lights in the cab. Get your weapons, prepare to defend me."

"Oh, right," Trayvan nodded quickly. "Like... this?" He cut the cab lights and took up position facing the doors, shotgun in hand.

"Shoot anyone who comes inside," Meelah ordered. She had no idea if he was a decent shot or not, but anyone coming into the cab was going get blasted, and that was fine with her.

She checked her pistol and the curving knife that she'd concealed inside her skirts. She knew, more or less, how to use both of them. She'd seen enough movies before to get the idea, anyway.

She would be damned if she let that idiot Fuller take the train away from her.

***

"There's the train, Captain," Brian announced.

There were no lights and some part of Jack wondered if the worst had already happened.

Even as he thought that, though, he saw someone with a flashlight rushing down the side of the train. Somone was alive, at least, so maybe they weren't too late.

"Let's go," He had already told them his plan, such as it was. Bail out, move up on the train, and take it back from whoever had control, and get it moving. He could worry later about reasoning with people. If that green fog and the things inside it reached the train, they would all die.

He stepped out into the downpour, the rain rattling off his armor, and he strode forward, the others fanning out behind him.

He saw people, soon enough, a half dozen armed men and women who formed up on the deck of the train and around the front engine.

"You ain't Fuller, who are you?" A voice shouted at him as he closed the distance.

"I'm Captain Jack Zamora," Jack snapped in reply. "Now get the hell out of my way."

The people there stood uncertainly as he continued forward. Off to the side, he saw more motion and Brian turned his truck's spotlight on someone struggling through brush towards the parked trucks. *Why are they all the way over by the trees? It's impossible to guard them that far out.*

Even as he thought that, he heard a sharp scream.

The woman going for the trucks had fallen afoul of... something. Something that looked like a ball of roots that rose up out of the brush, vine-like arms exploding up out of the bushed to wrap her up and even over the rain, Jack could hear the wet crunch and dying scream as it wrung her body like a washcloth.

Everyone froze, staring in that direction, and then looming out of the woods came the green fog and moving forms. More of the overgrown possessed lumbered out of that fog, followed by tall demonic trees and more of the vine horrors.

"We have to get this train moving, defend the train!" Jack called out.

"Screw this, I'm outta here," One of the men in front of him shouted. He sprung up and opened the cab door.

A gunshot sounded and the man's lifeless body toppled over the railing. The others guarding the train scattered.

Jack cursed under his breath and ran for the engine.

***

"Uh, was I supposed to kill him?" Trayvan asked as Marrik's lifeless corpse tumbled back out the open door.

He'd taken her orders too literally, but Meelah didn't care just now. The shining knight, armored from head to toe and seeming to glow in the headlights from the truck, was straight out of her nightmares. Her people scattered in his path as he charged for the engine.

"We need to run, come on," Meelah barked.

She rushed out of the door jumped off the back of the engine platform and onto the ground on the far side of the train. The rain pounded into her, she could barely see. She didn't know if Trayvan had followed or not. She didn't care.

She paused there, though, torn, looking up at the engine, at her chance to rule.

She pulled her pistol out, hands trembling as the armored knight reached the top of the ladder above her, light gleaming off his armor.

The tattoo on her chest burned and she found her hand lifting on its own, her fingers tightening as she centered it over the knight.

There were no thoughts in her head, it was as if the spirit of her former master filled her, all rage and hate and death. She aimed the pistol at the center of the knight's chest and she fired.

\*\*\*

Jack heard something, almost like a cry of warning.

He heeded it, diving for cover as gunshots rang out, bullets whipping past like malignant wasps. He moved into the crew cab, staying low, but flipping switches and turning everything on as he moved.

There was more gunfire outside, as rain or not, the things were coming at the train and people realized that they had to stop them or at least slow them down or they were all going to die.

Thankfully, no one had switched the codes and the diesel engine rumbled to life. Normally they were supposed to let it warm up before they put it under load. As a demonic tree flung one of the parked recon trucks out of its path, Jack figured they could worry about that some other time.

He put power towards the electrical motors of the train, the engines stuttering and rumbling as the power load almost choked them out.

The train lurched, wheels whining on the metal tracks.

The train lurched again. Larry climbed up, hacking at something out of sight. "There's some of those vines growing all over the wheels, it's bogging us down!"

"Get in here, keep us moving, I'll deal with that," Jack ordered. He went out, jumping down and, with the light from Brian's truck, he could see what Larry had meant. Vines had grown up and around the train's wheels and undercarriage. "Cut it free!" Jack bellowed.

People were out all along the train now and they looked over to him, standing in his armor and hacking at the vines. "Cut the train free!"

"It's the Captain, he's back!" someone shouted.

"Do as he says, or we're all dead," someone else shouted.

Someone had opened up with the machine gun, firing tracer rounds right over Jack's head and into the oncoming horde of demonic plants. Jack didn't look back at them, he slashed at the vines that held the train, even as Larry fed more power to the engine.

He had to trust his people to do the right thing. Right now, he had to get the train free or they were all going to die.

***

Meelah didn't know how she'd failed to kill him.

In the moment before she pulled the trigger, the light had flashed off his armor and dazzled her eyes, throwing off her aim. She'd emptied her pistol magazine and by the time she fumbled a reload, she realized she had missed her chance.

She had run, then. Trayvan ran with her, seeming confused.

The knight was the Captain. It seemed impossible. Impossible that he had lived, impossible that she had missed, impossible that he had come back.

Yet her world had unraveled. Once more, she was as she had been before Nidal Malik had found her, she had nothing, no food, no water, no followers... *nothing.*

The tattoo on her chest burned fiercer and she scratched at it. She heard a whisper, a voice.

*Failure... apostate.*

"What was that?" Meelah gasped as she continued to run. She didn't know *where* she was running, so much as away.

"I didn't say nothin," Trayvan answered.

"Not you... *him*," Meelah snapped. "Nidal." No that wasn't right. This wasn't his voice. This was his master's voice. This was *Meslamtaeda*'s voice, she felt certain of it.

*Apostate.*

The burning sensation from her tattoo flared up and Meelah let loose a panicked yelp as her skin felt like it was on fire. She ripped open her sodden dress, peering down at the blue tattoo, the flaming skull that Nidal Malik's people had worked into her skin when she swore loyalty to him and his god.

In the dark, the blue took on a glow.

"Uh, are you okay?" Trayvan asked.

Meelah couldn't talk, the burning fire sensation worked out from the tattoo, only it wasn't a warm fire, it was cold, painfully cold, a chill that made the falling rain seem warm in comparison. Her chest locked up, she couldn't breathe, couldn't scream. She dropped to her knees, her jaw opening in a scream that wouldn't come as the tattoo flashed with light.

*Failure... useless...*

The words were utterly alien and horrific, to the point that they made her mind writhe in psychic pain every bit a match for her physical pain.

Then, as she hit a point that she thought she would literally die, it cut off.

*Sacrifice.*

"Miss Meelah, are you okay?" Trayvan asked.

She understood the meaning of the word. With terrible certainty, she knew what her god wanted. She understood, now, that she had never truly been free of him. *Meslamtaeda* owned her. It had owned her since the moment she had sworn herself.

She had failed to kill his enemy, failed to destroy the train that had felled his priest.

She now had a choice, to give him a sacrifice or he would make her suffer in ways that made this attack seem as nothing.

All of Nidal Malik's words came back to her, his preaching about their new god, his power, his majesty, and how the holy dead were his servants.

She looked down at the pistol in her hands. Death would not release her, it didn't matter where she went, what she did. Meelah had sworn herself to *Meslamtaeda*'s service, body and soul. Everything she had done, it had been his will.

She was nothing. It hadn't been her who took over the train, it had been his will.

She was his slave, just as she had been Nidal Malik's slave.

Still, there were pleasure slaves and there were work slaves, and if she had to choose, she knew which she would be. She raised the pistol and shot Trayvan through the face, unable to miss at just a few feet away.

As his body dropped, she invoked the prayer of sacrifice, "Lord *Meslamtaeda*, take this offering, body and soul, in your holy name."

As she finished, the world around her flared in terrifying blue light, blinding her.

At the same time, an awful chill flowed through her, numbing her flesh.

As her eyes adjusted, she found herself flying.

*No, not flying... falling...*

She hurtled through *someplace*. Ancient crumbling ruins streaked past her as she fell, the walls lined by struggling, warring figures. Figures out of a nightmare.

They struggled under the cold, blue light, fighting and screaming in tongues that made her mind recoil.

This was a war, a war in a place beyond her mind, where billions of struggling monstrosities fought among each other. Cold fire blue fire and glowing orange flared, gouts and explosions killing thousands of them, flinging them screaming into the void where she fell.

One toppled past her, ichor and organs spraying as it screamed, dying but unable to die, its bestial face one of mingled hate and horror as she fell past it.

One horror beyond the next flashed past her, the scenes increasingly disjointed as everything she saw overwhelmed her senses.

Then, opening below her fall, she saw a portal open, like a toothy, flaming maw, and she was flung from that place and back into her world.

She struck the hard ground, her bones breaking and her flesh pulping. The impact should have killed her, should have driven the live out of her shattered body.

Only a new horror took hold as more blue light flared around her. Her bones snapped back into place, her flesh healed. She screamed in agony as her bones knit back together, her ruptured organs repaired themselves, until she lay, mewling in terror and pain upon the ground.

She was alive, her master had saved her, but in the most awful way possible.

*** 

Someone got the second engine going and most of the vines were cut away. The remaining ones ripped free as the train lurched again, this time the jerky motion turning into a continuous crawl.

Jack heard shouts and cheers. He didn't have time for that, not as he turned around and saw the wall of green fog towering above him.

Brian had pulled to the other side of the train and Jack didn't begrudge him that, there was no room for him to drive on this side.

The Ma Deuce roared, tracer rounds spearing into a demonic tree as it lumbered towards them, ripping off vast chunks of it and setting it ablaze until it toppled, burning and skidding to a halt just a dozen feet from the train itself.

"Left, on the left!" Someone called.

A vine horror exploded up out of the brush, tendril arms exploding outward. One snatched up a defender, vine growths wrapping him from head to toe in a heartbeat.

Jack rushed forward, swinging his blade into the limb with a shout.

The blade bit through and the man dropped, shouting. Two of his fellows ran forward to pull him clear, while several more used spears to drive the thing back.

Even as they did, though, lumbering plant-possessed had reached the train.

"Don't let them breathe on you!" Jack called a warning.

Green fog boiled off them, spouting from their growths.

"Hit them with fire!" Jack called.

Fire hadn't worked on the other possessed, though. They didn't have Molotov cocktails or flamethrowers ready. A couple people grabbed torches, waving the burning brands in the downpour, the flames sputtering.

A plant possessed corpse ran at him and Jack leaned forward into the thing's charge, delivering a powerful kick to its chest that drove it of its feet and jarring his body all the way up his spine.

"On the train!" Jack called, even as it started moving quicker. He slid his blade in its sheath on his back without looking and rushed towards the train.

He helped a fallen man up onto the engine ladder and then joined him. As the train backed down the tracks, picking up speed, the fog and foes began to fall behind.

"More of them!" Someone shouted.

Jack looked down the length of the train and he spotted the vine horrors as a pair of them crawled aboard the middle of the train, tentacled arms flailing at the defenders, flinging people off the train.

He climbed up onto the engine and then leapt from the back of it onto the next. As the train rolled, he ran, jumping from one car to the next, the rhythm of it coming back to him. He had fought on this train for months, he and his people had drilled on this surface, so that even in the pouring rain he knew the feel of it under his feet. Five cars down, he picked up a spear that someone had dropped and jumped to the car with the two vine horrors.

There was no time to think, he simply drove in at the first one, bringing the spear in low and driving it into the mass at the center of the thing with all the weight of his body and then shifting that into a lifting motion.

The spear drove into it and the thing flipped up and out over the edge of the car. Tendril arms flailed in an attempt to catch hold of something, but all it managed to do was swing down, under the wheels of the car. Several thousand tons of rolling steel did the rest as the wheels ground over the thing and Jack turned to face the next of them.

This one sensed Jack and tentacle-like arms flung out at him. He batted one away with the blade of the spear, then another, but a third caught the shaft and ripped it out of his hands.

Jack reached back and drew his blade, chopping down at a reaching tendril and severing it, black sap spattering out from the wound. The vine horror lashed at him from the side in response. Jack stepped into the blow, driving the blade in at the juncture between its tendril and the bulbous body and a thick stream of sap sprayed out.

The thing body-checked him backwards and more tendrils came at him, one catching his right hand and squeezing. His armor held, though, and he twisted his wrist, raking the blade down the tendril that held his arm and severing it, then hacking down to cut the one that had caught his leg.

The demonic plant, half of its limbs damaged or severed, came at him yet again. This time, though, it was off-balance and leaking its fluids everywhere and as it bore down on him, Jack moved to the side and it toppled over the edge, the mass of it falling between the cars and spraying fluids as the train ground over it.

The fog and possessed and nightmarish plants fell behind as the train rumbled back down the tracks. Someone on the train let out a ragged cheer and others took it up.

Jack just stood there, looking back at the attackers that still mindlessly followed them, at the limp bodies of those who had fallen fighting their attackers.

They had lost people. They would need to backtrack to Cuba, and then get on the right track. They still weren't out of danger.

But he had retaken the train and for now, that would have to be good enough.

# Chapter Fifteen

"HOW ARE WE LOOKING?" Jack asked as he climbed down off the train, once again in Cuba, Missouri. *Two steps forward, three steps back,* he thought to himself.

"A lot better with you here," Tim Kennedy limped up.

He and several of the other survivors looked rather the worse for wear. Jack gestured at his friend's leg, "You alright?"

"One of Miss Meelah 's people didn't like me asking questions." Tim told him. "I'm just a little bruised, is all. Brockman got roughed up as well, though nothing permanent, thankfully."

"Not everyone was so lucky," Jack pointed out softly. "Do we know how many we lost?"

"Not yet, I'll start taking stock, should we get everyone down or..."

"We're too close to those damned woods," Jack told him. "As soon as Brian and Larry get the tracks switched over, we're pulling out." They had backed the train out of the dead-end line and onto the main line again, they should just need to pull forward once Brian got the tracks switched over. That left them sitting in the dead, overgrown town of Cuba, but that was still better than the woods as far as Jack was concerned.

Tim gave a nod, though his eyes looked a little wild at the reminder of the attack. "What *were* those things, anyway?"

"I don't really know," Jack admitted. "Some sort of demonic plants, like the demon tree that attacked me." He frowned then, "That reminds me, anyone who got exposed to that green fog, or the stuff coming off the possessed, they need to get checked out right away. James Ott took a face-full of it and he was dead within minutes."

"Shit," Tim blanched. "I'll get the word out right away."

Brian, over at his truck honked his horn three sharp times.

"They got the track switched over, get everyone loaded up, we're pulling forward," Jack told him. "Take stock of who we have, who we lost."

"I'll do that, and everyone has seen you back already," Tim called as he limped towards the train. "Thank God, Jack. I wasn't the praying type before, but I know I said one of thanks when I saw you back."

Jack didn't know what to say to that. Thankfully, he had to focus on getting the train rolling again.

He climbed up onto the engine and then stepped into the cab. Robert Brockman was there, and the former architect looked rather more battered than the last time Jack had seen him. His eyes were swollen almost shut and his nose had been broken.

"You okay?" Jack asked.

Brockman touched his nose, "Yeah... just don't ask me to talk much, breathing sort of hurts."

He moved to the train controls and Jack saw his friend had already begun spinning things up.

"We need to put some distance between us and these woods," Jack told him. "We'll roll through St James as fast as we can manage."

"Aren't there raiders there?" Robert asked.

"Right now, I'm less concerned with them and more about the stuff in the woods," Jack assured him. "Get us moving."

Brockman gave him a wave and Jack stepped out of the cab, climbed to the next engine and then onto the train proper, even as the train engine rumbled into life.

Paul Meehan sat in the machine gun nest there on top of the first car. "How we looking?" Jack called. They had steel plates and sandbags up there to armor the position. Jack had the feeling they were going to need all that.

"We burned through two boxes of ammo back there," Paul called back.

"That was you on the M2?" Jack asked.

Paul nodded. "James and I..." He shook his head, "We trained on it after we got them from Malik's people. I gave some of those plant bastards a bit of revenge for James's sake."

"That you did," Jack clapped him on the shoulder. "I'll try to get someone else up here to support. We're going through St James, soon, and we are going to have to deal with the raiders when we do."

"Roger, Captain, we'll fend them off," Paul nodded.

Jack walked back along the train, swinging down into some of the cattle cars to talk with people, to reassure, assess, and at times commiserate about fallen friends and companions. Most of what he was doing was showing them at he really was back.

Everyone seemed almost painfully grateful for that fact. Tim's enthusiasm, if anything fell far short of what Jack saw from most of the other survivors. He didn't know if their gushing relief, often in the form of tears and even hugs, was a product of their rescue or if they really were that happy to see him.

It didn't really matter, he supposed. He went from the front to the back, not staying in any one place for more than a few minutes. He patted shoulders, shook hands, and accepted the occasional hug and moved on.

Along the way, he directed defenders to their posts, made sure the weapons that they had were distributed, and warned everyone that they were going to have to bypass the raiders to make it to the relative safety near Rolla.

At the rear engine, he found a couple of survivors, including Chris Peck manning the rear guard post on the train, overlooking the rear engine. "How are you all doing?" Jack asked.

Chris looked down, "Really glad you're back." He looked up, "I'm sorry, Captain, I... I voted for going south. I thought you were dead and..."

"Hey, Chris," Jack clapped the man on the shoulder, "A lot of people voted for it, you aren't the only one."

The former construction foreman didn't look up, "It was... horrible. Those plant things. We lost people and..."

"It is in the past," Jack assured him, not really sure about that. Even as he said it, he heard a shout and then a horn honking.

Looking over he saw Brian's truck pull up, the big man shouted and pointed behind the train.

In the darkness, at first, Jack didn't see anything, just the ground and grass swaying in the wind.

Except there wasn't any wind, the night air was still. And it wasn't grass.

Jack's eyes widened as he realized it wasn't the grass or even the ground he saw... it was a mass of undead, racing towards them. Thousands, possibly tens of thousands, coming down from St. Louis and the northeast, running along the tracks.

"Man the gun," Jack snapped, even as he pulled out his radio. "Robert, Tim, get the train moving, *now.*"

One of them said something over the radio, but there was a rumble of thunder that drown out their reply.

"Man the gun," Jack repeated. He looked around, his eyes struggling in the dark to make sense of what he saw. The wave of possessed were close, running down the tracks, a tide of undead flesh that would swarm the train if they didn't get moving.

The rumble of thunder grew louder and at first Jack thought it would crest and fade, only it didn't. The train car under him swayed and he thought, for a moment, that they were moving, finally. Only they weren't, they still hadn't moved.

"We need to go, now," Jack called over his radio. Again, he couldn't hear the response.

The ground trembled and shook still more and the train car actually *bounced*.

Brian Gnad's spotlight swung around to the trees and he honked his horn again. He hadn't needed to; some part of Jack's mind had determined that the noise came from that direction and he had already looked that way.

Trees swayed and shook. One fell, dropping down in front of the horde of possessed. Another fell, this one dropping into the horde of them, crushing dozens.

The entire wall of trees shuddered, swayed, and then fell as a mountainous mass drove through. It was forty yards wide or more, like a moving hillside. Trees shattered and spun end-over-end as it passed through. It went right into the mass of possessed, rumbling over their ranks, scouring them away like a colossal broom, then sweeping back through. Brian somehow kept the huge thing in the spotlight and Jack could see undead tangled in its mass of vines, even as it tore them apart, peeling back dead flesh and bones, consuming their corpses as they struggled.

Jack keyed his radio. "Robert, I don't know what the holdup is, but if we don't get out of here right now, we're dead."

The wheels started to squeak and the train trundled into motion.

They had backed into Cuba, waiting for Brian to switch the tracks over, and now they rumbled forward again, pulling away from the mountain of carnivorous vegetation. It shifted course, rolling right over the top of an overgrown building, flinging bricks and supporting beams away, sweeping up more of the mindless possessed that piled into it, then it swept back up the tracks.

"Should... should I shoot?" Chris Peck asked in a terrified tone.

Jack didn't want to provoke the thing; he wasn't even sure if the fifty-cal machine gun would do *anything* to that monster.

"No," Jack told him. "Until it comes at us, hold your fire."

"Look at the tracks," one of the defenders gasped.

Jack could see, in the light from Brian's truck, that where that thing went, it peeled back everything: rocks, trees, even the soil down six feet or more. That included the rail tracks, too, Jack could see, ripping and bending the metal beams as if they were nothing.

A green haze of spores swept off it, settling in its wake. Jack knew the origins of the terrible plant possessed, and the awful green fog.

It swept back around, drawn by the tide of possessed, or maybe provoked by their presence.

The train began to roll faster, even as the thing crushed another building, flinging an abandoned pickup truck a hundred feet or more before it tumbled out of sight.

There was no fighting something like that, it was a moving tide of destruction and Jack wanted his people as far away from it and the other flesh-eating plants as possible. "Keep an eye on it," he called as the rumble of the train grew louder.

"What do we do if it comes after us?" Chris asked.

"Call it up on the radio and open fire," Jack told him.

"Do you think this will stop it?" Chris patted his weapon. His eyes had gone so wide that Jack could see the whites all around.

*Not a chance,* Jack thought to himself.

"We'll stop it, if we need to, right now, let it fight our other enemies," Jack answered. He turned away, then, jogging down the train cars, headed for the front of the train.

When he got back to Engine One, he found some of his command team there.

"What if they damaged the tracks ahead of us?" Tim asked.

"The tracks were clear when Brian went through a couple of days ago," Jack answered. "There's no going back, now."

"Is there something back there?" Robert asked.

"Yeah, let's just say we can't head back north, okay?" Jack told him.

"What if they did something in St James between then and now?" Tim asked with a frown.

"Then hopefully Brian will spot it as we roll through and warn us in time to do something, otherwise it'll be a rough day," Jack snapped. "Look, put on the speed and we really need to *move.*"

Tim didn't seem to know if he were joking or not.

Then again, Jack really wasn't sure, either.

"We can't go back," Jack waved in the direction of St. Louis. "We *have* to get away from those woods," he waved south at the dark trees that loomed ominously, far too close for his comfort. The one colossal mound of vines had emerged; he suppressed a shudder as he imagined another exploding out of that wall of trees. It was big enough it could derail their train, rip the cars apart, consume his people every bit as easily as it had the possessed behind them.

"We have to go through St James. There are friendlies... well, *mostly* friendly, people in Rolla," Jack told him.

"You talked with them?" Tim asked dubiously.

"I talked with their leadership. And Josh has talked with them as well," Jack reassured him.

Tim scowled at the mention of the officer. "He abandoned us."

"He got me out of here, when Meelah would have probably cut my throat," Jack pointed out.

"Maybe if he had —"

"I don't know what went down in that vote," Jack held up a hand. "I do know that this Meelah person took over... speaking of, any sign of her?"

Tim shook his head, "No... none of her key people, either. A few of her thugs made it on the train again, there's discussion about throwing them off as we go past the raiders."

"None of that," Jack snapped. "If they did crimes against our people, I will deal with them. We're not going to get in the business of lynch mobs."

Tim didn't quite meet his eyes, though he gave a nod.

149

"Who was this Meelah person, anyway? The name isn't familiar," Jack asked in a distracted tone, his eyes still searching the trees as they swept along, his mind still on the thought of another horror coming at them out of the trees.

"One of the rescues we pulled out of St. Louis," Tim answered. "She said she was one of Nidal Malik's slaves, but the way she started acting when she was in charge, I think she might have been one of his people."

"She might have been, hopefully if she's back there, she's not anyone's problem anymore," Jack waved at the woods. His face went somber and he looked at the chalk board. There was a number, there: <u>1808.</u>

*Fourteen hundred and thirty-four of those adults, three hundred and sixty-four kids,* he thought to himself. He looked back at Tim. "How many?"

"Minus the people that went with you, we're missing thirty-nine," Tim answered in a quiet voice. "Meelah and her people are fifteen of those, Fuller and his truck went forward to scout ahead, so they might show up —"

"If they went deeper into the woods, then they are dead," Jack told him in a flat tone.

Thirty-nine lives. Sure, some of them had not been the best of people, some had probably even deserved death. But they were *his* people, his responsibility.

He wiped away the number on the corner of the board and updated it: <u>1769.</u>

"How are we on equipment and supplies?" Jack asked in a hard tone.

"We lost pretty much all the recon trucks and the gear and weapons on them," Tim shook his head. "Meelah had everyone park them well away from the train because she didn't want anyone else slipping away after Josh and his lot left..."

Jack shook his head. The loss of the recon trucks was more significant than he wanted to consider. Those trucks and their crews ran scouting missions out around the train, pulling in useful salvage and supplies. They might be able to replace the trucks and thankfully they didn't have to replace the crews.

The equipment and supplies on those trucks, though, that had taken months to assemble, each truck had weapons, tools, and supplies that allowed them to clear debris off the tracks, conduct repairs, breach into locked structures, and to allow the teams on each truck to survive on their own for days or weeks, if necessary.

"What else?" Jack frowned as he considered the efforts they would need to make to replace all of that equipment and supplies.

"Meelah had her people consolidate a lot of the supplies and weapons, we're still trying to find where she stashed some of it," Tim shrugged. "She pushed all of us out of the first car, took that over for herself and she moved the wounded and orphans out of their cars and put her people there."

Jack scowled at that, that first car had been for the families of his core team, the people that kept the train functioning. That had been necessity as much as anything else, he had to protect them. The hospital car, where their sick and injured were cared for and where Jack had been after his injury, had been car number two, the second-best defended car.

The car full of orphans had been the next one down, with the kids inside protected as much as possible. There were far, far too many kids who had lost their families. Some got adopted by other families, but until that point, Jack had them in the most guarded area of the train.

"We'll need to get them resettled," Jack frowned. That was going to have to wait until they cleared St James, though.

"Anything else?" Jack asked, looking between them.

"It's really good to have you back," Robert told him.

Jack shrugged. "I am sorry I wasn't able to stop the crazy bitch from taking over."

"It's my fault," Tim said in a tired voice.

"Both our faults," Robert spoke up. "We thought people would see sense, would vote with logic and reason, but..."

"She convinced people to vote her way, with bribes for more food or better spots," Tim shook his head. "They were bragging about it after it happened, and before we knew what was going on, she had armed thugs in various spots. Then Wachope bailed on us..."

"He got me out of here when I couldn't defend myself," Jack reminded him.

"Still, if he had stayed, maybe him and the other Soldiers could have —"

"Have what?" Jack interrupted. "I heard from him what happened with the vote. Rigged or not, if he had moved to remove her or forced the train to continue on, we could have had the whole train at odds, maybe people shooting each other, and the people who supported Meelah would have screamed about a takeover."

Tim looked down. "I shouldn't have pushed for a vote."

Jack wanted to tell his friend not to beat himself up over it, but he couldn't. Things had fallen apart without him there. He had to make sure it didn't happen again. "Look, if this has shown us anything, it's shown that we can't run this by committee. I've been running the show; I could die five minutes from now. The important thing is that we have a clear chain of command, that *all* our people are onboard with that. If I go down, Josh Wachope is in charge."

"He's not *you*," Robert Brockman protested. "You listen to people, you're military, sure, but you don't just snap orders and expect them to be followed."

Jack frowned, "Josh has plenty of experience..."

"He wasn't *leading* us, he was directing," Tim chimed in.

Jack scowled, but he didn't have time to argue further. "Look, we're going to be hitting the outskirts of St James in a few minutes. We're going to have to focus on the raiders there, first. We'll figure out what happens *if* I die later, alright?"

The two gave him nods.

"Alright, I've got to go, keep us going unless Brian signals there's a problem with the tracks. We aren't here to fight a battle, just to push through, got it?" Jack told them.

Robert gave him a nod and Tim a thumb's up.

Jack turned away, determined to figure things out as best as he could.

***

"What's it look like, Brian?" Jack asked over the radio as the train trundled along through the growing dark. They were right up on the edge of town as best as they could tell, and there was no stopping now.

"Pitch black," He answered. "They could have done a lot of damage to the tracks in the past couple of days if they wanted."

It was a serious risk, especially since they still didn't know if Meelah or Fuller had worked out some kind of deal with the raiders who controlled the remnants of the town.

"Take the lead," Jack ordered. "If you see something, try to give us as much warning as you can." It wasn't like they could go back, anyway.

"Will do," Brian's voice was tense, and Jack couldn't blame him. They were driving into the unknown, but he didn't dare stay here on the edge of the woods, not after seeing the army of demonic plants that had attacked the train. He wanted his people safe, or at least as safe as possible. He would risk the raiders over the horrors in the woods any day.

They came around the last curve and the only thing he could see was the lights from Brian's truck ahead of them and the light of the train.

"Do you think they hear us coming?" Robert asked nervously.

"You know what, if they don't..." Jack reached over and pulled down the train horn, the loud blare of it loud even in the soundproofed cab.

"We're giving them warning?" Tim protested.

"If they didn't hear the rumble of the train, already, then we'd be lucky. We might as well approach this with as much confidence as possible," Jack answered. He moved to the back door. "I'll be on the deck, watching for threats. Keep an ear on the radio for Brian."

He didn't wait for any response. Outside, it was far louder, the rumble of the train hammering him, even at the relatively low speed.

Jack didn't know if they would make it, didn't know what kind of defenses the raiders might have put in, whether they had cut the tracks or had heavy weapons capable of disabling the train.

Still, between the demonic plants and the raiders, he would take his chances against the raiders.

***

Eddie Needle felt a jolt of panic as the wailing noise cut through the night.

"What the hell was that?" Cutta asked. Cutta was jumpy, but the woman cooked their meth and she had a habit of sampling the merch. He did too, for that matter, but not as much as she did.

"It's just the train," Eddie told her. He couldn't shake the uneasy feeling all the same. His sentries had reported seeing the lights. They knew it was coming.

The collapsed world that he had lived in was many things. Violent, for one. And he liked that, how he could take what he wanted and do what he wanted. Simple, too, in that if he tried to take something from someone stronger, meaner, or tougher, they would probably kill him.

This world wasn't *loud* though, and the wailing horn of the train was *loud* in a world that had gone mostly quiet. There weren't planes flying overhead or the rushing of trucks on the highway. There wasn't the sound of trains thundering down the tracks, either, until now.

There was something primeval, as he heard the wail of the train horn and the rumble, something that shook Eddie, and he saw it in the expressions of his gang.

"Get out there," He snapped at them. "They think they're just gonna roll through; we're going to take their train, take all they got!"

That wasn't enough, he saw that. He didn't have Jazzy here, she'd gone south to scout and hadn't come back yet, and while the gang listened to him in her absence, they *feared* her.

He drew his machete and advanced on them, men and women scrambling back from him. "Anyone who ain't out there cracking heads is gonna get the chop, understand?"

They backed away from him. That damnable train horn blasted again, closer.

"Bobby, you take your bikers down Jefferson Street," Eddie snapped. The big main road would give them plenty of room to move up on the train and then they could run next to it and board.

"Myles, you lot go down Merrimac Street, get on board the middle of the train and see if you can get hostages," Eddie pointed at the group. Mac grinned at that, because that was how they had got into the high school here, taking some of the farmers hostage and threatening to kill them if the others didn't open up.

"Trev, you four with me, we'll go down to Carson Street, where they'll have to slow down for the curve," Eddie grinned, "We'll get on board the engine."

He looked around, Jazzy wasn't here, but he knew how excited she would be if they could seize the train. "Anyone with guns, lay down some fire on them, get them to keep their heads down so we can get onboard."

"What if they shoot back?" Cutta asked.

"Then shoot the ones shooting back," Eddie snapped. "This ain't different from the farmers we took here."

"This school wasn't rolling along," Bobby whined.

"They won't be once we stop them, and then we'll have all their stuff, too," Eddie snarled. "Now, get out there, move it!"

*** 

Jack moved up to the front of the train, able to see better without the glass and lights in the cab. The train lights lit up the big modified snow plow on the front and beyond that, the tracks and area around them. They bore down on the town, Jack's heart beginning to race as he thought about all the ways this could go badly wrong.

155

Brian's truck rolled through the first train crossing spot, a hundred feet ahead of them. A moment later, gunfire rippled out from on top of the building overlooking the railroad crossing.

Jack didn't know if they were shooting at the truck or the train, he didn't wait to find out, either. "Gunner, one o'clock, infantry on the building roof." He called it over his radio.

"Engaging," The Browning M2 on the roof of the lead car opened up, the roar of its gunfire loud even over the rumble of the train. Tracers and bullets lashed over Jack's head and scythed through the upper area of the building.

"I think I got them," Paul Meehan's voice sounded rather cheerful over the radio.

Jack kept quiet, wanting to keep the chatter to a minimum on their radios.

He spotted some headlights coming down from a side street. "Vehicle approaching, three o'clock, I don't have eyes on."

"I got nothin," Paul answered.

"Trail?" Jack asked.

"Uh, I don't see them," Chris Peck answered over the radio. That wasn't too much of a surprise, at fifty-five cars long, he was well to the rear.

"Anyone else have eyes on the vehicle?" Jack asked.

The radio was quiet for a long moment. The train continued to rumble onward. They went through another intersection; Brian's truck passed the main street and the downtown area ahead of them.

"This is car twenty, I've got a group of motorcycles or dirt bikes, lights off, on approach, right side." The voice on the radio was excited.

Jack's head snapped around and he leaned around, trying to see in that direction. They didn't have lights all the way down the train and the track curved a bit, so he couldn't see them.

"Status?" Jack asked.

"They're coming along side, oh, crap, they're boarding," the radio call cut out.

Jack swore under his breath and jogged towards the back of the engine. With the speed they were traveling, the train shifted around under his feet more than he liked.

He heard gunfire, then, too, and jumping up onto the roof of the engine, he saw muzzle flashes as defenders fired at their attackers.

He wanted to sprint down that direction, but he also had to trust his people to handle it.

The engine trundled across the main street crossing. More gunfire ripped out from a position down the street and this time, Paul Meehan didn't wait for the order, he returned fire, the M2 loud from this close. Jack saw the front of that building dissolve under the impacts.

\*\*\*

Eddie swore as gunfire ripped overhead and some more of his people died. Jazzy was going to be really pissed with him, but *she* was the one who had left.

Maybe she had left because she knew this was coming. If so, maybe he should deal with her when she got back. She always let him be the one to take risk, maybe he should do something about that.

He rushed forward towards the train, just as it slowed on the curve and he and the men with him jumped for the ladders and chains on the side.

One of them missed and Eddie heard his scream cut off with a wet squelch as he fell between the train wheels. Eddie grinned to himself, though, as he climbed up.

He was going to take the train, take their guns, take their supplies.

The wealth this train represented made the risk worth it.

\*\*\*

Jack heard a shout, and he turned as three raiders came up over the *left* side of the train car, one of them leaping on Paul Meehan. Jack rushed them, his feet steady on the moving surface of the train. He drove a kick into the face of the man who had Meehan down, feeling the impact all the way up his leg as the raider toppled backwards and over the side of the train.

One of the raiders swung a baseball bat into Jack's side, but it bounced off his armor with a clang. Jack drove his armored elbow into the raider's face and the man stumbled back and then fell screaming off the side of the train. The third raider, looking between Jack and Paul, realized he was outnumbered.

"You pricks messed with the wrong gang," the man growled, even as he backed up.

"Seems like we dealt with your friends well enough," Jack told him.

"Well, the name's Needle, and I'm going to get mine back from you," the man spat at him, flipped him the bird and then jumped over the side himself.

Jack rushed over and saw the man had leapt onto the roof of a parked car, and he sprinted off into cover before any of Jack's people could shoot at him.

Gunfire still crackled through the town and a bullet ripped past Jack, close enough that he ducked down behind the sandbags of the gun position.

As they cleared the final intersection, the gunfire dropped off.

Jack checked his radio, "Status?"

"This is car twenty, we drove them back," came the answer.

"Trail car," Peck announced, "we just passed the lot of them, looks like they're down or out."

Jack felt the tension in his stomach begin to ease. As Brian's truck went under the overpass and the train followed, he gave a last look at the town. They'd cleared it, there was nothing between them and Rolla, now.

He had led his people clear of the trap.

# Chapter Sixteen

THE TRAIN RUMBLED ALONG, a slow, steady crawl that put distance between them and the raider town. They would reach Rolla around dawn, at this pace. They could have gone faster, but Jack didn't want to push things in the dark.

He stood in Engine Two's cab, staring out at the darkness beyond the windows, wondering what other threats lay before them.

He felt a tremendous relief in that he had recovered his people from the carnivorous plants and led them past the raiders in St James. That relief was tempered by the fact that those threats weren't gone, they lay behind them.

The raiders and the plants and the possessed. Three different, *radically* different, threats.

He *almost* wished that one or the other would deal with the raiders for him, though he didn't know if he would wish the fate of being consumed by carnivorous plants or turned into a soulless undead upon even the scummy raiders.

Light had started to appear upon the horizon behind them. Dawn approached.

"Captain, I've got lights ahead, looks like two trucks," Brian called on his radio.

A moment later, he heard a squawk on the cab radio, "Train, this is Doc, come in, uh, over."

Jack recognized Katie's voice. He stepped past Robert Brockman and took the radio, "Glad to hear you."

159

He signaled Robert, "We'll stop, I'd like you back on board."

It wasn't a fast process, but with the raider town behind them and Rolla and unknowns ahead, he was content to stop the train and let his people onboard. Their two trucks pulled up alongside and Jack jumped down.

Before he could even head in their direction, though, Katie rushed him, almost tackling him in a hug. "God I was worried."

"Nothing to worry about at all," Jack lied. His mind went to the horrors in the woods and the raiders and the army of possessed.

"Phew... you smell like rust, sweat, and rotting plants," Katie stepped back a bit. "Still in the armor?"

"I hadn't had a chance to take it off," Jack shrugged. If he were honest with himself, the thought of peeling it all off with how tired he felt really didn't appeal. "Everything alright here?" His gaze went west, and he wondered if her being here was because she'd been threatened or afraid for their safety.

"Yes, actually, Doctor Arden has been a model host. They've consolidated most of their people down on the college campus, as it is more defensible. I guess that's how she ended up as their leader, her doctorate is in agriculture." Katie told him. "They've begun tearing down other buildings, both for materials to build defenses and for metals and other resources they need."

"Hmm," Jack kept his mouth shut on any aphorisms, such as "those who can, do and those who can't, teach."

"They set us up in a guest building, we had the place to ourselves and no one bothered us," Katie went on.

"That's good to know," Jack's concern had been that their new 'friends' might betray them and hold their people hostage. It didn't look that way, not just yet, at least.

Jack's mind went to the threats behind them, "We need to get moving again," He called out to the others. He looked at Katie, "Are the tracks clear?"

She gave him a nod, "Yes, like I said, they've torn down buildings to make defenses but they cleared out the ones blocking the railroad tracks after we got there. They have a *lot* of people, it's actually jarring, I have to admit, to see so many people in one place."

Jack nodded. He led her aboard Engine Two, giving a wave at Robert Brockman in Engine One to show that he could get them started as soon as everyone was aboard.

Inside the cab, he pulled Katie close to him in a hug and he let some of his fear and worry wash over him. It was a lot, almost too much, and he found himself letting go and moving over to the window, to stare at the darkness beyond.

"It will be okay, love," Katie told him as she came up next to him, taking his hand.

Because she was there, because this felt like the first alone time they had, he spoke, his voice distant. "I had a dream, love. Of a woman."

"Should I be jealous?" Katie asked in an amused tone.

Jack shook his head, "No... it was nothing like that. It was when I was injured, I felt like I was dying and then I was in a cold, dark, place. Only the darkness eased and there she was. A woman, a *lady,* wreathed in light... glowing."

"Glowing?" Katie laughed. "What, like an angel or something?"

Jack looked over at her, his expression somber, "Is that too far of a stretch?" He gestured out at the darkness beyond the glass, the first light of dawn starting to ease the darkness, "With what we've seen, is it too much to think that there's something good out there, too?"

Katie didn't say anything in return. She squeezed his hand, though, showing that she appreciated his point.

Jack closed his eyes, "I could feel her, light and warmth... she said that she *needed* me."

"What happened then?" Katie asked in a small voice.

"She lifted me up, away from the darkness," Jack shrugged. "The nightmares eased and when I woke..."

"You were healed," Katie nodded. "It didn't... it *doesn't* make any sense. You had broken ribs, blisters and burns on your body from the sap of those plant

161

things, I think you had internal bleeding, too." She shuddered, "I was certain I was going to lose you. But your breathing eased, and then a day or so later you were up and around."

Jack nodded. "She healed me."

"How... why?" Katie frowned. "Nidal was healed by the Hand of God —"

"The nightwalker," Jack corrected her absently. "I refuse to call that thing anything to do with God."

"Sure," Katie nodded, "but it doesn't change the fact that it healed Nidal, it gave him back the use of his legs after years of him being unable to walk. It didn't just heal his nerves, it had to have repaired atrophied muscle and tendons, too. If one of those things can do that, how do we know this glowing woman isn't more of the same?"

Jack shook his head, "I don't know. Just a feeling."

He closed his eyes again, seeing the soft features, feeling the warmth that she radiated. "There was coldness and death with the nightwalker. Nidal Malik was cruel and power-hungry. I get nothing like that feeling with her."

"Okay," Katie nodded.

Jack looked at her, and he could see in her eyes that she wasn't entirely convinced. "I'm not crazy," he assured her.

"If you are, at least you're my kind of crazy," Katie laughed.

Jack laughed with her. It felt *good*. They were alive, they had rescued his people. Sure, there was a hostile military officer with what might be an army to deal with. There were still hosts of the possessed. There were raiders and demonic plants and all kinds of other threats and horrors in the world beyond.

For now, though, they were alive. They were together. That was enough.

\*\*\*

Meelah wasn't quite sure how she was still alive. After she had sacrificed Trayvan, she had fully expected her god to abandon her. Instead, she had been thrown

162

through what, as far as she could tell, had been hell itself, only to end up here, broken and battered. Then he had healed her, made her whole again.

The experience had been so overwhelming, so terrible, that it took her hours to do more than uncurl from a ball. It took her a little while to figure out where she was, looking around at the buildings, trying to make sense of things. That was, until, down the street, she caught a glimpse of a big, silver arch.

*St. Louis... I'm back.*

The sun had long-since set and she clutched her arms around herself and shivered a bit. She was still soaked from the rain in the woods. The heat of summer didn't bake away that chill, though. It was a chill, a coldness that seemed to permeate her.

Looking north, at where flames still billowed in an angry glow, she had a terrible premonition.

Those flames began to dim and the summer night crew chill. She could feel it coming.

A dull red glow of the northern part of the city, still aflame, illuminated its arrival.

Meelah fell to her knees before the thing. *Nightwalker.* The title came to her, even as she put her face to the ground, her pulse hammering in her ears. "My lord."

"I am *Meslamtaeda*'s new emissary to this place," The thing's terrible voice made her head ache. "He has saved you, so that you might serve him."

"I am glad to serve," Meelah forced the words out, through a mouth that felt dryer than dust.

"You shall be his priestess, where Nidal Malik failed, you will succeed... or your suffering will know no end," the Nightwalker told her. She had a vision of the terrible place, the place where things like the Nightwalker struggled against other terrors every bit as bad or worse.

"Are you the Hand of God?" Meelah choked the words out.

The Nightwalker did not answer for a long moment. "That is the name of my predecessor. A hand can be open or closed, can give and can take."

The terrible voice, like nails on a chalkboard and rocks grinding against one another seemed to bore into Meelah's skull. "I am not a hand... I am *Meslamtaeda*'s Wrath. You may call me Wrath."

Meelah shuddered at the being's terrible words. "Of course, Wrath. How may I best serve our god?"

"You will find the others sworn to his service and recruit still more. I want an army. Of the living and the dead. We will crush this spark of resistance, the *train*, and their Captain."

She shuddered again at the malevolent *hate* in his words, the force of it seemed to almost peel back her skin.

She didn't want to go back to the train. She didn't want to serve this terrible being. The tattoo on her chest burned, though, and the sick, cold feel of her master's attention bore down upon her. She had no choice. She did their will or they would destroy her utterly.

Meelah was a survivor. She would do what she had to do to stay alive, and if it meant killing every man woman and child on that train, she would do it without hesitation.

"Your will be done, Wrath."

***

"How did they escape?" The thundering voice demanded.

The priestess shuddered, "Mistress, I do not know."

"They hurt, even killed many of my offspring," her goddess's voice made the steel platform vibrate.

"They were going to your offspring," The Priestess told her. "To the heart of your woods."

She hadn't even had to influence them to do it, they had been doing it on their own. Only now, with their leader back, they were coming towards her people, and that might well bring her goddess's wrath with them.

"I want them, I will feast upon their blood and flesh," Her goddess demanded, the voice echoing up from the great cavern below, making the entire platform rattle.

"I will deliver them to you," The Priestess promised. "I swear it will be done."

"If you do not, then you and yours will be my feast," the voice below shifted, the tone almost petulant. "I *hunger*."

"I will feed you, my goddess," The Priestess gulped, well aware of the danger. The horrors that her mistress could unleash often would not distinguish between her followers and other targets even under the best of times. She had few illusions about what would happen to her people if her goddess decided to feast upon her people instead.

"Bring them... or do not return," the voice below echoed.

The Priestess took that dismissal and hurried up the ladder and away from the cave. She would have to move quickly, not only to appease her mistress but to strike before the train's survivors knew who to trust.

She paused as she reached the top, her gaze going up to the clouded night sky, her eyes searching the dark above her for some glimpse of familiar stars or light, some bit of hope in the darkness.

It was a vain effort, she knew. There was no hope in this world.

THE END

*The story will continue with Hell Train 3*

# About the Author

Kal Spriggs is a writer of science fiction and fantasy stories with over 30 books in print. An avid reader, he started reading J.R.R. Tolkien, Andre Norton, David Eddings, and Robert Heinlein in the 2nd grade and a love of reading and good stories has been constant with him ever since.

Kal is a graduate of the United States Merchant Marine Academy. He followed in his parents' footsteps and joined the US Army after graduation and served as an active-duty engineer officer, a reservist, and as an active reservist. He is a combat veteran with deployments to Iraq and Afghanistan. Kal has a master's degree in environmental engineering and has worked in civil construction and environmental remediation.

His enjoyment for seeing new places has been facilitated by his career choices, and he's been to over thirty countries. Kal likes hiking, fishing, and skiing, and his favorite places are typically in the mountains of Colorado. His other hobbies include wargaming, tabletop RPGs (both as a DM and player), metalworking, and just about anything else that takes his interest.

A father and husband, Kal and his family live wherever the Army tells him to (he doesn't often get much choice in the matter) but he thinks of Colorado as home.

His website with more information, details on upcoming books, other random things can be found at kalspriggs.com

Kal's Amazon Page

# Also by Kal Spriggs

*The Shadow Space Chronicles*

The Fallen Race

The Shattered Empire

The Prodigal Emperor

The Sacred Stars

The Temple of Light

Ghost Star

The Star Engine

The Centauri War*

*The Renegades*

Renegades: Origins

Renegades: Out of the Cold

Renegades: Out of Time

Renegades: Royal Pains*

*The Star Portal Universe*

Valor's Child

Valor's Calling

Valor's Duty

Valor's Cost

Valor's Stand

Valor's Inheritance
Valor's Strike
Valor's Uprising
Valor's Exodus
Valor's Liberation*
Lost Valor
Stolen Valor
Hidden Valor
Common Valor
Forsworn Valor
Loaned Valor
Maligned Valor
Bound Valor*
Fenris Unchained
Odin's Eye
Jormungandr's Venom

### The Eoriel Saga
Echo of the High Kings
Wrath of the Usurper
Fate of the Tyrant
Sorcerers of the Black Fortress
Prophesy of the Dark Moon*

*Forthcoming

# More from Cannon Publishing

**Join the Crew!**

SIGN UP FOR OUR newsletter for the latest news on new releases and more.

# Follow our authors at their Amazon Pages!

Shane Gries (Dragon Finalist)

Lucas Marcum

Al Hagan

James Copley

Jason Kyle

G. Scott Huggins

Michael Morton

Charles Hackney

Jon LaForce

Jason Weiser

Kal Spriggs

Brian Gifford

Charli Cox

Dan Kemp

Jonathan Shuerger

J.R. Wise

Steven Vickers

David Hensley

# More Books from Cannon Publishing

## Irregular Scout Team One

In July of 2016 a plague swept the world, and the civilization collapsed and fell. For a lone National Guard sergeant, a veteran of the wars overseas who had settled down to a new life, the nightmare began on a hot summer evening at the barricades. Orders and chaos, gunfire and being overrun, his unit dwindles away in the face of the infected. Months later, living in the ruins, the thud of helicopter rotors followed by a crash and the rescue of a downed pilot leads Sergeant First Class Nick Agostine back into the arms of the US military. From his experience comes the idea of teams, military and civilians experienced in dealing with the undead and barbarism of the wilds. The first Irregular Scout Team leads the way for Task Force Liberty to advance down the Mohawk Valley in Upstate NY, making contact with survivors and clearing out the infected with stealth and firepower.

*Volume 1*

*Volume 2*

*Volume 3: Civil War*

*Volume 4: Bad Company*

*Volume 5: End of Days*

# The Line

When the world descends into chaos and anarchy with an unbelievably swift plague, turning victims into ravenous maniacs, the soldiers of America's storied 1st Infantry are asked to hold the line. From the brutal streets of urban combat to the bloodied, desperate defense on the plains of Kansas, they fight a war against an unrelenting enemy who used to be their fellow citizens. As civilization falls, can they hold the line?

*The Thin Dead Line*
*Dead Storm Rising*
*The Big Dead One*

# Fallen Empire

What's a soldier to do when the war is over? When he's only known conflict his whole life? Since time immemorial the solution has been to find another war, this time for pay. Whoever has the credits and wins the high bid gets the experienced fighter. Sometimes, though, the credits aren't enough to cover the price. Empires rise, but Empires also fall. The Terran Union has spent five centuries under the control of the alien Grausians, like a barbarian tribe under the thumb of Rome. Now, after almost two decades of civil war and succession struggles, the formerly subject races have settled back in their ancient territories to lick their wounds and re-arm, leaving hundreds of settled planets to exist in a political vacuum. Into that space steps the free companies, mercenary units that fight for gold, honor, power and glory. Veterans who can't get the wars out of their souls, new recruits looking for adventure, corporations with their own agenda. Join us in a 27th Century that echoes history.

*The Irish Brigade*

*Overrun*

*Silent Violence*

*Doom Company*

*Dirty Deeds Trilogy*

From Book 1: Sandy Decker had a problem. Well, multiple problems. Some good, some bad. Some pretty bad. The good problem is that she was up a whole bunch of credits and the title to an Azelia class yacht called Vagabond King. That was the good problem. The bad problem was that she was in debt to Daresh An-Jaska, Former Princeps in the Golden Legion, Grausian exile, and the biggest gangster in the sector. Not a money debt but a favor debt, one that she paid principle on doing favors in return. Dirty deeds that never seemed to pay enough, of course. That was until yesterday, when she found a line she couldn't cross.

Today, faced with a brutal and violent death at the hands of Jaska, Sandy did what any good former spy would do. She told a story and sold a secret. Operation Marconi and the missing Terran Union battleship *U.S.S. Resolute*. Now it's good news, bad news.

The good news: Jaska bought the story.

The bad news: Jaska didn't trust Sandy as far as she can throw a grat. So the mob boss put 'controls' in place to ensure her compliance. The kind that blew your head off if you didn't do the job.

Now all Sandy and the crew of the Vagabond have to do is follow a decade old trail to the *Resolute*, salvage the mission package for Operation Marconi, and find the objective—a secret location where the Old Empire produced their greatest weapon.

*Vagabonds: A Fallen Empire Novel*

# Athenaeum, Inc

The Professor has problems, and not just what decades of soldiering did to his back and his knees. His boss just died, leaving him as CEO of the extremely discreet intelligence contractor Athenaeum, Incorporated. His old buddy the Operations Director is a highly skilled Army Ranger veteran but his finance chief is slightly unhinged and spends her money on highly inappropriate work outfits. The surviving old men on the Board of Directors are stuck in the 1970s. Running Athenaeum out of an old Cold War bunker and keeping their roster of experts together is expensive, but the government contracts are drying up or going to bigger, flashier corporate players.

*Door Number Three*
*Doubling Down*

# Off World

When nuclear war erupts on Earth, the American colony in the Alpha Centauri system is left stranded. As the new day dawns, a furious attack by the native inhabitants threatens to overwhelm the colony's defenses. It's left to the thin red line of the US Army's 9th Regiment to stem the tide and ensure humanity's survival in this harsh new world. From two time Dragon Finalist and author of the best selling series "Irregular Scout Team One" and "Invasion" comes a new tale that tells of the struggle for survival on a brutal planet.

*Offworld: Ragnarok*
*Offworld: Expeditions*

## Cannon Fodder: Tales From the Gun Crew

Fifteen stories from Cannon Publishing Authors, each taking from the universes of their novels to bring you perspectives and deepen their world. From 27th century mercenaries fighting on distant planets and young soldiers riding with Arthur to defeat Saxon hordes, to enchanted weapons dealing damage in hands of Fae, we bring you the best of Science Fiction and Fantasy!

# Valkyrie

Humanity engages in a desperate struggle with an alien species for this side of the Orion Arm. Space ships die in instantaneous bursts of light and turn into vapor, but on the ground Marines scream and lie wounded in the mud and blood, praying for the Valkyries to come save them. They aren't wishing for death and a Nordic goddess to take them to Valhalla, the wounded are praying for the men and women of the '348th Field Hospital MEDEVAC to dive through fire and hell to come save them. Because they know that ...Valkyries never die!

Valkyrie
Valkyrie: Rebellion
Valkyrie: Attrition

### *High Caliber Awards*

The Cannon High Caliber Awards are an annual contest for new writers. In it we ask them to submit a novella length story of Science Fiction, Military or Fantasy genre to challenge their skills.

2024

2025

# The Wishkiller Saga

While on patrol Captain Aethal Paaling discovers evidence that an ancient terror has reached the rich soil of his home: the Lotus, a prolific growth whose addictive leaves devour their victims from within turning their hosts into horrible, terrifyingly violent mockeries of humanity. Created at the dawn of history by the twisted power of a godly relic called the Well, the return of the Lotus may be a harbinger of even more horrors to come. Carrying the fatal news to the capital, Aethal discovers that even in the face of death itself, the Lords Paramount of Verlaen will fight to keep their secrets and their power. With only the guidance of his legendary Greater Rifle and the aid of the Pheonix Lancers, the soldier must find his way through the halls of a forgotten holy order and into deep dens of crime seeking answers. He must find the truth as quickly as he can, because the Lotus may have already taken root among those he loves... and fighting it may cost him everything, including his soul.

*A Cold and Mortal Spring*
*War of the Shattered Moon*

# *Hexen*

When nine out of ten people in the world have died in a brutal plague, what do those who remain do to pick up the pieces? Does the creed, "Duty, Honor, Country" have a place any more if there's no country left? On his way across the devastated remains of Texas, Marine Corps veteran and survivor Eric Marten rescues a young woman from a vicious attack by men who have turned into savages. As Dani slowly learns to trust him, they try to stay alive in the deathlands that America has become, using all their wits to survive a post-apocalyptic nightmare.

*90% Death Rate: A Post Apocalyptic Thriller*
*Angel of Death: A Post Apocalyptic Thriller*
*The Bloody Princess: A Post Apocalyptic Thriller*
*The Devil's Pitchfork*

# Hell Train

**A single train carries what might be the last vestige of civilization through a hellish nightmare.** A few hundred alive out of millions, lights going out all across what was once America as the possessed arose from the dead and murdered the living. A few hundred survivors travel across the country in an armored train, seeking some place to shelter in a fallen world. All that remains is a dystopian nightmare marked by rains of blood, impossible horrors, and portals to Hell opening in the skies.US Army Captain Jack Zamora is responsible for their safety, a self-imposed burden that wears on him every day. Fighting off undead, protecting the survivors, keeping the train running and supplied as his team desperately plans their next moves. Starvation and disease threaten. but it gets worse, because the ancient gods have sent their emissaries, horrific beings of myth and legend that walk the Earth. Things that can drain a man's very life essence or even that of an entire city.

*Hell Train: All Aboard*

## The Path

**Sometimes a hero isn't what you expect, and the one you need comes from the castaways of society.** Nearly broken and at the end of his rope, former decorated scout pilot and prisoner of war, Red has finally accepted the inevitable. He and his kin have no future in the Human Confederation of Worlds, being gene mods and barely human themselves. With the help of his friend he flees Terra for adventure and fortune out in the reaches of the galaxy. Along the way he's dragged back into conflict that calls on all his piloting skills and he learns the deeper meaning of Kin, as his crew becomes his family.

***Path to Freedom: The Path, Book One***

## Invasion

More than a decade after the Confederated Earth Forces were defeated, their commanding general, a boyhood protegee, lives in exile and disgrace. His life on an isolated farm is forever changed when two strangers show up at his homestead, and the war comes crashing back down on him. The problem though, remains the same. How do you fight an enemy that is technologically superior and holds the high ground?

Invasion: Resistance

Invasion: Day of Battle

Invasion: Total War

## *Military Sci-Fi/Fantasy Anthology*

The military experience is timeless, and echoes down from our past and into our future. Along the way, not everything is as it seems. Thirteen stories from established and new writers in the field of Military Science Fiction and Military Fantasy bring you tales of the terrors of combat and the even greater fear of the unknown in Cannon Publishing's first Bi-Annual Military Anthology.

# The Hundred Worlds

Fifteen classic Science Fiction stories from both masters of the craft and up and coming new writers! A tyrannical United Nations pulls the strings of its colony worlds, ruling with an iron fist. Corporate interests take precedence, and brushfire rebellions smolder on the edges. One system, home to the only alien species yet discovered, with human allies throws off the yoke and calls itself Independence.

# MECHA

Feedback from the slight pressure of a hand closing sends a powerful mechanical arm smashing into an opponent. A neural link hurls blustering plasma fire from your suit's shoulder mounted cannon. Your reactor levels scream with overload as return fire smashes into your armor, and damage alarms wail while you hurl your twenty ton body sideways for cover. You're a Mecha, a mechanical fighting machine with a human pilot. The guy that the infantry curse at in training and pray for in combat. The machine that the last hopes of your people ride on. The construct that strikes fear deep into alien hearts as they hear your turbines power up. The one able to pass through hell and come out the other side victorious, or die trying.

*Under A Different Sun*

In the near future, massive empires rule the stars, and west of the Reach, they are battling for control of new systems. In the no-mans land between the front lines, Captain Nate Meric and the crew of the privateer Lexington fight for prize money, and loyalty to their ship and their friends. Beneath it all, though, runs a hidden dream. To see America restored, and take her rightful place among the stars.

## *Sea of Fire: Demonrise*

Brian Corel, former slave, gladiator, ex-fiance to an Empress, exiled Captain of the Taland Royal Guard and now owner of the frigate *Widowmaker,* does the best he can to balance the lives of his crew with his own desire to live life as a free man. Skirting the border between being a privateer and an outright pirate, Corel stumbles into a war with a religious cult intent on corrupting the kingdom of an old friend and has to set things right while grieving over his lost love. Along the way he signs a dragon into his crew and has to risk everything to rescue his brother from the grasp of a demon that has destroyed an entire continent.

## Chosen by the Sword

**There are some things a PhD doesn't prepare you for, like running two feet of steel through the guts of a flesh-eating monster straight out of a nightmare, while ducking razor sharp claws. Or having the sword critique your fighting style while you do it.** Dave Howard had a problem. Last week, he was out looking for a teaching job in the middle of a wrecked job market. This week he was neck deep in green blood and hellfire. Dragged into it by the very sword, his grandfathers' mysterious possessed blade, that was now walking him through hacking up a ghoul without getting his own head cut off. This wasn't exactly what he had gone to school for, and the University he had just taken a job with seemed to be anything BUT an academic institution. More like some kind of monster hunting bunch of weirdo nerds. Maybe his degree in Personality Psychology might be useful there, at least. The fighting though ... as he dodged another swipe of claws and awkwardly tried to follow the instructions the sword was screaming at him, he shot back at it, "Hell, I'm Canadian! Swordplay isn't in my cultural DNA!"

## *Beyond the Wall: A Novel of Post-Roman Britain*

**The legions are but a memory, the glory of Rome only a shadow of crumbling ruins and broken walls.** A darkening tide of barbarism was washing across Britain's shores and the lights of civilization were slowly flickering out into darkness, only kept burning by the legendary Red Dragons cavalry unit. Led by their Tribune, Arthur, who serves no kingdom but goes where the fight is hardest and most crucial, they wage desperate battles to keep back the tide. The Red Dragons ride the length of Britannia to fight the invading Saxons, Scoti and Picts, wherever they show, from across the seas or down from the Highlands. At sixteen years old Peredur of Gwynedd has listened all his life to the stories of his father Pelinor fighting with Ambrosius Aurelianus. When word comes that his older brother has been slain in battle with the Saxons, his desire for revenge leads him to follow in his father's footsteps as a warrior, becoming a cavalryman with the Red Dragons. Along the way he may either find himself a warrior and leader worthy of Arthur or be left lying forgotten in the dust of history.

# Hell's Bells: War & Love Downrange

Two souls collide in the middle of a deadly war.

Sergeant Sylvie Lyons of Her Majesty's Royal Engineers wishes she'd listened to her grandda's advice and stayed away from the military.

USMC Sergeant Hondo Cassidy wants nothing more in life than being a Marine and fighting. Hondo and Sylvie find themselves thrown together when his artillerymen are assigned to provide security for her engineers deep in the desert of Afghanistan.. Amidst death, destruction, cultural misunderstanding and the inevitable that happens when you mix an all male unit of Marines with an engineer unit that is mostly female, Sylvie and Hondo find in each other a reason to live. That is, if they can survive.

# Semper Die

**The dead rose expecting a feast. What they got was a firefight.**

Sergeant Alex Slaughter and the Marines of Alpha Squad were on a routine training exercise near Quantico when everything went silent. No comms. No command. No clue.

What they find when they return to base is worse than anything they trained for: a bioweapon has unleashed a zombie virus that has shattered civilization, and now they must survive the Collapse.

But as the squad pushes deeper into hostile territory—through the death-choked streets of Arlington and into the rot-stained corridors beneath D.C.—they discover that the undead aren't the only threat. Desperate survivors, rogue military units, and darker truths buried beneath the weight of secrecy will test their loyalty, their mission, and their very humanity.

Written by USMC veteran Jonathan Shuerger and set in J.F. Holmes's brutal and unrelenting Irregular Scout Team One universe, Semper Die delivers pulse-pounding action, authentic military detail, and a terrifying vision of what happens when duty and apocalypse collide.

**Lock. Load. Semper Fi. Semper Die.**

*Semper Die*

*Esprit De Corpse*

## *Troll Hunter*

**In a world ravaged by endless war between humans and trolls, Gabriel Cullen, a grizzled hunter gifted with the rare ability to track by scent, is captured by the very creatures he hunts.**

Bound both by his captors' chains and by an ancient prophecy, Cullen glimpses a chance to end centuries of bloodshed—if he can trust the trolls who butchered his kin. When a sinister force from the deep dark threatens both sides, and even trolls tremble at its approach, the tracker is forced to question everything he believes.

Unaware of her father's changes in hearts, his daughter, Isabo, a fierce warrior driven by duty and vengeance, vows to rescue him, leading an army that wields a devastating new weapon to crush the troll clans. Yet her quest risks igniting a deadlier war. As Cullen allies with a young troll warrior and a blind shaman to confront a demonic evil from a forgotten age, both father and daughter face wrenching choices between peace and betrayal.

In a land where hope is fragile and blood stains every blade, their sacrifices will forge a new world—or shatter it forever. Troll Hunter is a raw, gripping saga of loyalty, loss, and the brutal cost of survival.

# More From the Fae Wars

## Get the full series!

### *Onslaught*

What would you do if America and the world were invaded tomorrow by a relentless and brutal enemy? In an alternate 2015, a US Army Special Forces Team, part of the legendary black ops unit "Delta", is in midtown Manhattan to take out a Chinese spy and his handlers, sending a message short of outright conflict. All goes smoothly until they find themselves in a full blown shooting war through the canyons of the City. Portals from another world have opened in Central Park, making a way for figures out of historical nightmare to invade. The Fae, creatures banished from Earth thousands of years ago and now only part of our legends, have returned with Dragon fire, spell and sword to conquer and take revenge. The first volume of The Fae Wars covers Team Three, G squadron, Special Forces Detachment (Delta) as they fight their way off Manhattan and then join the defense of the refugees as the Fae assault the bridges. The fabled 69th Infantry puts up an epic fight against superior weaponry and then the war descends into the asymmetric hell that the Delta Operators know so well. Along the way they find new allies and old powers that come to their aid.

### The Fall

For the first time in two hundred years an enemy has stepped foot on American soil and war has come to our cities. The US military is rocked back on its heels and driven into a fighting retreat as each defense line falls. The foe is unstoppable and ... Fae. Creatures from a legendary past who have come to reclaim the Earth in the name of magic and revenge. In the hills of Pennsylvania a ragtag, devastated army prepares to make a last stand against dragon fire capable of melting an Abrams tank and wizardry that stops fifth generation fighter jets in mid-air. Inevitably it comes down to shining steel verses human will, and Sergeant Oliva Acevedo transforms from a hospital clerk to a hardened fighter. Volume Two of the best selling "Fae Wars" follows the fighting retreat of the US Army as the Fae establish control of a shattered America.

### Futures Past

Two thousand years ago the Fae were banished from Earth and they've spent that time plotting return and revenge. When their portals open around the world and start crushing the human's military with spell encased steel and dragon fire, it becomes a massive struggle between technology and magic. When the Fae Invasion hammers the West Coast, Captain James Powers and his California Army National Guard artillery battery is caught on its way home from Annual Training. In a running battle the unit is smashed by combat with orcs and elves, leaving their commander struggling to keep his people together and alive. Along the way a dying priest with a strange ability to see the future manipulates people and events to bring Captain Powers to his true calling as a Seer. As they run and fight, the humans gain new allies, Fea tinkerers who love all things mechanical and hate the elves. With their help they begin to take the war to the enemy in a brutal mayhem of ambush and assassination. Book Three of the Fae Wars series following the bestselling "Onslaught" (set in NY City) and "The Fall" (Pennsylvania)

### Tales From the Occupation: A Fae Wars Anthology

Wars end, enemies are defeated and territories are conquered and the combatants have to return to a life changed. America and the rest of humanity have fallen to the Fae, ancient mortal enemies of mankind. After building their strength for two thousand years, the Elves have claimed their vengeance and now rule Earth with an iron fist and dragon fire. Down but not out, a human resistance is building, but first daily life needs to be lived. An anthology of stories exploring life during the Occupation in the best-selling Fae Wars universe.

### Insurgent

*Wars come and wars go. Eventually even the most belligerent of combatants will arrive at some kind of living arrangement, either through exhaustion or slaughter. Kill enough, down to the last child, and there will be no more war ... until the next one, of course.*

In August 2015, the war started, portals opening up between their world and ours, allowing the Fae to return to our (or their) home world in blood, fire and magic. Conventional forces fought back as well as they could, but the invasion had been planned to hit us in the middle of our civilization. America's military was scattered overseas or concentrated in large bases that were quickly overwhelmed by forces that were dropped right in the middle of their units. The fighting was brutal and horrific, magic overwhelming technology. It took six weeks, and the President surrendered to spare the civilian population. A puppet government was put in place and the Fae started to divide the conquered lands into principalities run by their Great Houses, slowly turning America into a land of feudal slavery. Thing is, though, the Fae had lived in their exile for thousands of years, fighting wars among themselves and against various races that populated their new home. Pitched battles where there was a clear-cut winner and loser. They had never fought an insurgency and had no idea how bloody it could get. Major David Kincaid. United States Army 1st Special Forces Operational Detachment–Delta, soldier of a defeated but unbroken nation, was going to show them. If, that is, he can keep the faith. The follow up novel to the bestselling "Fae Wars: Onslaught" by J.F. Holmes.

### Ghost

*There are wars, and then there's War. The all-encompassing thing that is fought on many levels, and with many kinds of weapons, many kinds of warriors. Even ghosts.*

Alex was no one, a man just trying to get by at his paperwork job at the new Homeland Security. A man grieving for his wife, who had died in the Invasion. Someone just trying to keep his head down while the elves appointed him to do the paperwork of putting their boots on the necks of a conquered American people. Thing is, even a nobody paper shuffling clerk has a weapon, one that had lit the fires of revolution in America hundreds of years ago. His mind, and his words. The internet was still up and running, somehow and someway, and Alex takes to his keyboard. Inspired by his hero Patrick Henry, soon the words of the "Ghost" start inciting attacks on the Fae and the District of Columbia rings with explosions, gunshots and cries of Freedom. The Resistance notices, and Alex is soon assigned a bodyguard and a handler, an ex-police officer who is running from her own hidden past. Together they work to keep the flame of resistance alive and escape from the tightening net of the Fae. The consequences are, as always, Liberty or Death.

### Northwest Front

Fae Wars returns on a new front as war rages in the Pacific Northwest!

Corporal Erik Doherty isn't some kind of special operations super soldier; he's just an infantry grunt trying to get by in what was once the United States Army, now an enforcement arm of the Fae overlords. When orders come down from a chain of command more interested in boot licking their new masters than protecting American citizens, he has to make the choice. To serve and live, or run and die? Ashleigh Greene is a teenage girl with a price on her head, the Fae looking for retribution for the killing of one of their nobles. As her hometown burns behind her, she flees into the mist shrouded forests of the Pacific Northwest, her family killed by dragon fire and her world destroyed. On separate paths, each human comes face to face with a haunting legend that has lived for thousands of years. One that has been waiting, watching, and hating the old enemy that has finally returned. Together, they bring war to the Fae in a battle for honor and revenge. Book seven in the best-selling Fae Wars series!

### Vendetta

The echoes of the Fae Invasion have died out in the Midwest when a new thunder rumbles across the plains. Tukor, former warband leader of the Red Arrow Clan, now rides with a motorcycle club of humans and orcs against his former masters. It's hard to tell which challenges Tukor more though; being the new chief of all the orcs in the free city of Wichita Falls, Texas, or being engaged to the tough and lovely human woman Misty.

Throw in an elven duke that's still pissed at Tukor for murdering his sons, a motorcycle club that'll follow the chief to hell and back, and a newly arrived orc matron determined to prove Tukor and Misty wrong about their future. The Fae occupation of the Midwest just got way more bloody.

Featuring orcs on choppers, magic ammo and a whole crew of Army SpecOps, the tale of Tukor and Misty is a front seat view of the occupation in the Southwest that no one expected, least of all Tukor himself.

### Relics of Empire

In a world shattered by elven conquest, where magic crackles and dragons soar, the Navajo Nation stands as a defiant refuge. Living there is Ben Yazzie, a battle scarred Marine veteran who wants no more war—until a brutal encounter with elven oppressors at a remote gas station ignites a spark of rebellion. Alongside Maria Hernandez, a grieving widow fueled by vengeance, and a band of unlikely allies, Ben is thrust into a fight against an empire wielding arcane power and ruthless ambition.

As ancient ley lines awaken, unleashing chaos across the American Southwest, Ben uncovers a legacy of resistance tied to his ancestors and a mysterious relic from a forgotten era. Magic surges and the earth itself stirs, forcing Ben to embrace his destiny as the Coyote, the elusive and mysterious warrior leading a desperate stand against an otherworldly tyranny.

From the dusty trails of Arizona to the neon-lit chaos of Las Vegas, *The Fae Wars: Relics of Empire* is a pulse-pounding tale of courage, sacrifice, and defiance against overwhelming odds. Will the old ways and a warrior's heart be enough to reclaim a shattered land?

The rebellion begins here.

### Harley's War

In the tale of years, counting from the day the Fae returned to Earth, the war was done in six weeks. Fighting stuttered on for two years afterward, as the Great Houses assumed control and built human society into their liking. Or ignored it. The shock troops and great armies of the King were withdrawn, to leave the conquerors, the conquistadors, to send back tribute to the Old World.

The Event, when the Demon Core made its presence known on this world, changed the nature of everything, allowing t he magical Paths of the Way to be accessed by Humans on the level of what they had known of old, before the closing of the portals in 528 CE.

However, throughout the ages between that date and the Event, despite the closing the Ways by the Magus Concilium, there have always been wild magic users. Some haunt humanities legends as heroes, some paid a high price and were burned at the stake. When the Fae returned and our technology failed, they were often the fire that kept our resistance burning. Hereafter is the tale Harely Osman, the woman who was to become famous as The Dragon Rider throughout the war-torn lands of a defeated county.

~ Major James Bognaski, Unit Historian, United States Army Mage Corps
Excerpt from "Spelljammer: The Corps Monthly"
Issue #271, Vol 1, August, 2046

### *More Tales From the Occupation*

Life is hard. Under the bootheels of an oppressor who cares nothing about human life? Almost impossible. Thing is, though, when you put the boot on the neck of Americans, they tend to get a little pissed off and a lot worked up. Doesn't matter if they face overwhelming odds, heavy firepower or bewildering magic. They're going to resist, to the death.

The Fae have won, and they're trying to do their best to beat that spirit of independence out of their ancient enemy, humanity. In a lot of places, people are just trying to survive, but here, there and everywhere someone, somehow, will stand up and say, "Not me. Never."

Eight tales of ordinary people, and some not so ordinary, fighting a war that they may never see the end of but never giving up.

# Authors

### John Holmes

J.F. Holmes is a retired Army Senior Noncommissioned Officer, having served for 22 years in both the Regular Army and Army National Guard. During that time, he served as everything from an artillery section leader to a member of a Division level planning staff, with tours in Cuba and Iraq, as well as responding to the terrorists attacks in NYC on 9-11.

From 2010 to 2014 he wrote the immensely popular military cartoon strip, "Power Point Ranger", poking fun at military life in the tradition of Beetle Bailey and Willy & Joe.

His books range from Military Sci-Fi to Space Opera to Detective to Fantasy, with a lot in between, and in 2017 two are finalists for the prestigious Dragon Awards.

In 2018, he launched Cannon Publishing, www.cannonpublishing.us specializing in military science fiction, fantasy and thrillers, with an emphasis on works from up and coming authors.

### Lucas Marcum

Lucas Marcum is a critical care nurse practitioner and an officer in the US Army Reserve. When he's not working, or performing his reserve duties, he can be found hiking, reading, attempting to perfect his soft pretzel recipe and spending time with his family.

### James Copley

James Copley is a former Non-Commissioned Officer of the U.S. Army, having served over twenty-one years in both Active and Reserve/Guard units, variously trained as Infantry, Communications, and Ordnance specialties before finally retiring from the Army National Guard in 2016. During his service, he deployed four separate times, twice to Iraq and twice to Afghanistan.

He is currently working as a software engineer in Central California with his wife, two children, and two dogs. Reading was his number one passion from a very young age, and more recently he decided to try writing his own. Feel free to join him on his writing journey!

## Charli Cox

Charli Cox is a best-selling Military Sci-Fi and Horror Comedy author. She also writes Sci-Fi, Alternate History, and Military Fantasy stories.

If you enjoyed Fae Wars: Northwest Front and want to see more stories about Ash and "Gunny," Cannon Publishing has you covered. Burnt Mountain and Sasquatch will be coming to your Kindle later in 2025. Also, please be sure to leave a review!

Representing #teamandmore, Charli's first published short story is in The Phoenix Initiative: First Missions from Chris Kennedy Publishing. She has stories in Bureau 42 and Express Elevator to Hell, also from CKP.

Look for Whistles of the Wendigo, an Alternate History/Military Fantasy novel set in the Joint Task Force 13 universe from Three Ravens Publishing, due to release soon.

Charli's previous experience has been as a Realtor, HVAC Business Manager, IT Office Manager, and freelance bookkeeper. Professional skills such as drafting strongly worded emails transition surprisingly well into writing fiction.

An animal lover and #boymom, she lives in SW Oregon with her Leg husband, two sons, an Arabian mare, and two Husky mixes who think they are hooman.

Learn more about Charli and sign up for her newsletter on her website. Hang out with her on Facebook, Instagram, and/or TikTok.

## Jason Weiser

Mr. Weiser has been a government contractor for the last eleven years, and before that, a writer working odd jobs trying to get by. He has a BA in History from CUNY Brooklyn. Mr. Weiser released his first novel in 2025, with Cannon Publishing, but before that, released a short story in their 2018 Spring Military Sci Fi Anthology.

Mr. Weiser is also an avid wargamer and has been published quite a bit in the hobby, having most recently run "Military Miniature" magazine as it's editor in chief from 2021-2023. Before that, he wrote for EpochXperience (a division of SJR Research) as a contributing writer for their blog on wargaming and military history topics from 2020 to 2021.

He also wrote two scenario books on Cold War wargaming topics, "Red Star, Burning Streets" and "Red Star, White Lights".

Mr. Weiser encourages all his fans to visit Cannon Publishing at their website

## Brian Gifford

A military veteran with more than 25 years of service in the U.S. Air Force and Army (in an order that would surprise you!), Brian is a lifelong science fiction and fantasy nerd of the highest order. A student of the hard sciences and the arcane arts of cybersecurity and IT alike, Brian has spent a lifetime accumulating his unique view of the world, which he now insists on sharing with everyone else. He is a husband in awe of the magnificence that is his wife and the proud father of three awesome sons, and looks forward to retiring from the military in the near future to focus on his family and his writing.

## ML McIntosh

ML McIntosh is a part time rock star, part time vengeful essence of femme wrath. She works the always shift in unapologetic science fiction, dream fiction and urban fantasy. Follow her Instagram @ml_mcintosh and stay weird.